A Civil General

A Civil General

David Sinebeck
and
Scannell Gill

SANTA FE

Sunstone books may be purchased for educational, business, or sales
promotional use. For information please write: Special Markets Department,
Sunstone Press, P.O. Box 2321, Santa Fe, New Mexico 87504-2321.

Book design | Vicki Ahl
Body typeface | Americana ▌ Display type | Edwardian Script
Printed on acid free paper

Library of Congress Cataloging-in-Publication Data

Stinebeck, David, 1943-
  A civil general / by David Stinebeck and Scannell Gill.
    p. cm.
  ISBN 978-0-86534-663-5 (pbk. : alk. paper)
  1. Thomas, George Henry, 1816-1870–Fiction. I. Gill, Scannell, 1943- II. Title.
  PS3619.T5646C58 2008
  813'.6–dc22

                                        2008012940

Published in
Santa Fe

WWW.SUNSTONEPRESS.COM
SUNSTONE PRESS / POST OFFICE BOX 2321 / SANTA FE, NM 87504-2321 /USA
(505) 988-4418 / ORDERS ONLY (800) 243-5644 / FAX (505) 988-1025

To Jared, Catherine, and Jeffrey
for their love and extraordinary patience

he authors are grateful to Captains William Stineback and John Beatty for their wartime recollections, to Edward Mullaney, Dorothy Reo, Raymond Smith, and Larry Mohr for their guidance on the manuscript, and to Judy MacKenzie, Teri Strahlman, Debbie Brandt, Manny Carreiro, Shalom Endleman, and Mary and Bert Mullaney for their support. For the general reader, this novel is largely factual in its battles and settings and imaginary in its encounters among real and fictional characters. We have attempted to remain true on every page to what is known of General Thomas' character.

The quiet, patient soldier, who from his first day's service in Kentucky had never swerved a line from the strict performance of his duty to his Government, according to his oath, without reference to self, had now met his reward. His fame had steadily grown and rounded from the time he gained the first Federal victory in the West, at Mill Springs, up to the battle of Chickamauga, where he saved the Army of the Cumberland to the nation. He had always been the main stay of that army, holding the command of the centre—either nominally or actually the second in command. Upon his judgment and military skill every commander of that army depended, and no movement was made without his approbation. Yet so modest was he that his face would color with blushes when his troops cheered him, which they did at every opportunity.... His kind consideration for the feelings of others was one of his marked characteristics. With a pure mind and large heart, his noble soul made him one of the greatest of Nature's noblemen—a true gentleman. The experience of Chickamauga ripened his powers and developed him to his full height. As the General who won the first victory in the West, who saved an army by his skill and valor, and who was the only General of the war on either side able to crush an army on the battlefield, George H. Thomas...stands as the model American soldier, the grandest figure of the War of the Rebellion.

—Henry M. Cist, 1882

Major General George H. Thomas

1

The woods are crashing. We sit on our horses as still as we can. If the branches cut by the minnie balls fall on us, they do less damage if we do not move, and they are falling everywhere.

But it is the noise not the branches that we notice. It is deafening. To make ourselves heard, even from two feet away, we shout at the top of our lungs. General Thomas never turned his head when he spoke in battle, and he spoke so deliberately that too much time—and noise—passed between words. What did he want us to do, Generals Baird and Brannan, and I?

We never expected this battle now. We knew there was going to be a fight soon. We were in Georgia after all, and the Rebs would not put up with that very long. But none of our scouts had alerted us to Confederates on the left. Worse yet, Old Pap did not have all of his troops to fight with. All he had were my cavalry and those two divisions. Maybe eight thousand men against who knows how many Rebs in the woods ahead.

A cannonball comes flying out of the woods in front of us, not fifty feet away. My horse rears and I start to topple off. I see the general as I go down. He moves his head six inches as the ball flies by, powdering on a rock another fifty feet behind us. He seems twice as large as I am, a perfect target with his barrel chest and regal bearing. But I am the one who falls.

I clamber back up, embarrassed in the midst of the fighting that a cavalry officer can fall off his own horse. The general has not even noticed, yet he seems to pause before speaking again until I am back in the saddle, sitting motionless next to him.

I hear him this time: "Go get Reynolds on the right!"

I wheel away.

This was Chickamauga, a little town in northern Georgia, just south of Tennessee. Whatever fame General Thomas got in his remarkable career, it was usually linked with Chickamauga, a battle he did not even win. But this was just the start of Chickamauga, not the last day when he held a line no other general could have held, while his commanding officer had already given up and ridden away.

This was the first day, the day that will always be clearest in my memory of him.

I get to Reynolds on the right, though I do not know how—dead reckoning, I suppose. Like the rest of our troops, he is spread out, not together. The battle has begun by accident, too soon, and no one is ready. It must be six or seven miles from one end of our army to another. But that does not scare the enemy at all since we are so thin up and down the line, so easily overwhelmed. All day long my cavalry dash to plug one hole after another, and Forrest's Rebs seem to be doing the same thing on the other side of the Chickamauga. Maybe they are not ready either. All I know is, it is chaos. Our men come into the fight as they arrive on the field, one regiment after another. First Baird and Brannan with me, then we are driven back and Palmer comes in, but his right gets turned. Van Cleve arrives to support Palmer and is thrown back, but Reynolds, after I go for him, reinforces and then is overpowered himself. Davis, Wood, Sheridan, Negley all rush in when they get there, and the fight is even as the sun starts to go down.

Thomas is steady on his horse the whole time. His young aides, Kellogg and Willard, sweat in their saddles as the battle rages in front of them. The day is long and dusty, the sun fierce in the sky. Men and animals are suffering from thirst, and the soldiers who have marched all day to get here have only one meal before sundown.

Then, when the general tries to move Baird's and my men back to higher ground for the next day's fight, the Rebels hit again. Confederate artillery fills the woods with shells that make the twilight skies seem like a firmament of exploding stars.

When it is over, we are almost where we began. It is eerie. Everyone is shivering in the cold autumn weather. Most of their blankets have been tossed away in the battle. The wounded and lost fill the hollows, huddling together.

At the height of that first day at Chickamauga, frightened horses run in every direction, and the dead and wounded cover the riverbanks. The dead bodies are piled upon each other to make room for columns heading to the front. And Chickamauga Creek is red with blood. I have never seen anything like it, and the battle at Stone River was bad.

That day, of all days, he did not win or even control the

fighting—it had a mind of its own, and a crazy one at that. He lost thousands of men to wounds and death on September 19th, 1863. It was not his finest hour, that had come a day later, or at Missionary Ridge in November, or Nashville the next year.

That first day, when he sent Croxton at the very beginning to capture an isolated cavalry brigade only to discover five or six brigades that our scouts had missed, and Croxton came back to the general and said, "General, I would have brought them in if I had known which one you wanted," Thomas just smiled and said nothing. He did not even seem disappointed. It was as if his mind was moving forward to the next task, the next maneuver. And Croxton, like the rest of us, knew how the general would react, that he would not throw a fit or criticize our failures. Croxton merely turned back to the front, to resume his work.

And there is another story about Thomas and General Sheridan at the end of that first day. They were sitting on a fence rail watching their exhausted men return to camp. Thomas seemed spent and said little or nothing about the day, one of the wildest of the war. When Sheridan made a move to return to his troops, Thomas suddenly offered him some brandy from a flask in his saddlebags. The orderly brought the flask and Thomas took very little, giving the rest to Sheridan—a man, by the way, who later curried favor with Sherman and Grant at Thomas' expense. Sheridan paused again, but Thomas still said nothing about the fight. And Sheridan rode off in silence. Then, a few minutes later, in my own presence, General Thomas took the hand of a passing private and thanked him for his valor and steady courage. The soldier's response was remarkable, especially compared to Sheridan's silence a half hour earlier: "George Henry Thomas has taken this hand! As good a man as ever was! I will knock down any mean man that offers to take it hereafter!"

We knew we were in the company of a great general—but it was more than that. We loved him, those of us who fought and died for him. If we fell off our horses, he would wait for us, patiently, to get up; or to return like Croxton; or to pass by like the private. He never lost sight of us for a minute.

He was the most successful general in the war, more than Grant and Lee and Sherman. But he is being forgotten—an injustice I must try to correct, twenty years after his death.

His life itself was unjust. His family in Virginia disowned him when he chose to fight for the North; his superiors distrusted him, and delayed his promotions; and he died defending himself against the scurrilous attacks of a fellow general.

I was a newspaperman before and after the war, so I knew the public followed his exploits and trusted him with their sons. He was revered for his victories, and for his determination to lose fewer men than the other side.

But his truest public recognition came only in death, when President Grant and his cabinet and a hundred and forty carriages of dignitaries met the train bringing his body from San Francisco to Troy, New York and accompanied the casket to the cemetery. No one from his family was there. But ten thousand other Americans were.

Perhaps he saw in us, his men, the expression of what he most wanted, to his own detriment. Some of the promotions he was offered he turned down. He refused to curry favor with politicians and generals higher up the ladder. His victories were tempered by the horrors of war. He always seemed alone. But before Chickamauga he took me into his confidence and I came to understand him. And that understanding changed my life.

2

I saw him for the first time on the last day of 1862, at Stone River, six months before Gettysburg in the East.

He had won the first Northern victory in the West at Mill Springs at the beginning of the year. But this was the first big battle in the Western campaign for Atlanta, and it was very big. Even with the fighting at Mill Springs and Perryville, the Union men who joined after Shiloh knew they had not really been in an all-out fight. They did not know what that meant; the battles in the Mexican War that some had seen were no bigger than Perryville.

We knew how large the two armies were that were facing each other in Tennessee, maybe fifty thousand men each. You would go see friends in other regiments and it would take hours to find them, passing through brigade after brigade. Of course, our generals always insisted that the Rebs had more men than we had, that they were defending their own slave territory in Tennessee, even if half the population still supported the Union. So we pictured how many men were out there and we could imagine what it might be like if they all flew at each other at once.

What we could never imagine was how completely out of control it would be when it finally happened, how totally subject to luck and chance the outcome would have been without General Thomas. Maybe that was his genius: nothing he did ever seemed to be a matter of chance.

At seven in the morning on December 31st, 1862, the cavalry regiment of Indiana boys I had organized in May approached Stone River on the edge of Murfreesboro, Tennessee. We were not yet part of the Army of the Cumberland. Rosecrans had asked for more cavalry assistance, since the Confederates were always running rings around our troops with Forrest's and Morgan's cavalry, and we were sent over from Carter's forces at the Cumberland Gap. As we got closer to Murfreesboro, we found the entire corps we were attached to—Thomas' corps—was moving forward like some giant machine with people as its working parts. As far as the eye could reach, both in front and behind, the road was packed with men. A dozen bands played martial airs, while the morning sun reflected off thousands of muskets and the air blew through hundreds of American flags. You would think we were all pushing, crowded, to some Fourth of July celebration at the next field over. It was cold, of course, but just the anticipation of something important happening made us warmer.

My four hundred men were walking their horses until it would get so crowded that, to save space for the infantry, we would mount up and get a clear view of the grand size of the forces we were sending into this first big battle to control the roads and railways to Knoxville, Chattanooga, and Atlanta. The country before us was unexplored by our side, and every ear was open to catch the sound of the first gun. The conviction that a big battle was coming kept the men steady and in line. You could feel their nervousness.

As we passed the fine houses and well-improved farms in the area, there were few white people to be seen. The Negroes appeared to have entire possession. I cannot speak for my men, but it raised my spirits to see such people in charge of their master's property.

A young and very pretty white girl stood in the doorway of one handsome farmhouse and waved the Union flag, a sympathizer perhaps or just trying to save her home. Cheer after cheer rose along the lines, officers saluted and soldiers waved their caps, and the band played both "Yankee Doodle" and "Dixie," as if to show that it did not matter what we played, we were going to take the day. That girl won a thousand hearts, men who would fall in battle that day, dreaming of her and home.

We turned a bend and a number of our East Tennessee cavalry were engaged in firing the houses along the roadside that had been abandoned by their disloyal occupants. They informed us that our troops on the right had already been surprised this morning by the enemy and routed. In their anger the Tennessee boys were doing the only thing they could think of.

Then we began to hear the rumble of the battle in the distance. Our pace imperceptibly quickened and we found ourselves trotting and veering down roads to the left, as if to stay ahead of the sounds moving in from the right.

As we approached the strife, the number of stragglers, refugees, and baggage wagons retreating in confusion so obstructed the road that we could barely make our way to the front, while the roar of artillery, the rattle of musketry, and the shouts of contending parties could be heard above the confusion around us— a scene calculated to try the nerves of veterans.

Then, less than a mile from the battleground, General Thomas appeared out of nowhere. One of his aides, Kellogg, was with him. Thomas stood straight in the saddle, his head slowly turning to take in the entire scene. I was no more than thirty feet from him on his right; he must have come up from behind. He always rode so quietly. He had not even seen me, I thought, but out of the blue he turned and said, "Colonel Swain, put your regiment in line of battle across the field on the left of this road, and I'll put that Pennsylvania regiment of infantry on the right, and somehow, persuasion, reasoning, or threats, we'll stop this stampede."

And he was gone, to some other spot, directing some other regiments he already knew.

We did what he said. Veering again to the left, we made our way through fields of corn stubble and thickets of cedar bushes. Out of a line of thickets we arrived within sight of one of those grand and terrific struggles that characterized all the great battles of the war, where foes met in an almost hand-to-hand fight, with a determination to conquer amounting nearly to desperation. Across a large field, drawn up in a semi-circle, long lines of mounted troops stood opposed to each other, firing their carbines and revolvers with a rapidity that caused a constant roar, over which thundered and reverberated the frequent discharge of artillery.

Suddenly, however, the firing in a great measure ceased, and our cavalry, my regiment included, with a terrific shout charged upon the enemy lines but were met with a firm stand and withering fire, before which our line reeled and was compelled to retire, which they did, however, in good order. It was just a feint of sorts to slow down the enemy, and it only worked for a few minutes.

General Thomas had moved his mass of infantry and cavalry gradually to the left, and up a small rise that approached the railroad line from Nashville to Chattanooga. Stone River and the Nashville Pike came in there as well, so he could oversee all movements of all troops, Union and Confederate, and the natural barriers that might halt them. Stone River was not deep, you could ford it on foot, but it would slow up the troops who crossed it. By nine o'clock the battle was in full swing, and you could not tell how our side was doing. Fleeing soldiers from our right side, McCook's division, were pouring into our lines, but they were meeting and joining new regiments, like mine, that were calm and ready, and placed just where General Thomas wanted us. So we somehow were not affected by the fear on their faces. It was as if they finished a race and were embraced by the officials who would tell them that it was all right, they tried.

The 14th Indiana, my regiment, was fighting on foot, firing over the heads of our on-rushing men when we thought we saw a gray uniform. With the tremendous smoke, though, it was hard to see clearly. You usually guessed how far behind the running blue uniforms the running gray uniforms would be. They still were not close, so we tried not to use up too much ammunition. Perhaps twenty thousand men, up and down a line in front of the pike and railroad, were facing the oncoming Rebs. This time it was Negley's and Rousseau's divisions, with the remnants of McCook's corps, rushing through the line and reforming behind it as best they could. The Confederates had already pushed back McCook's troops at least a mile. Sheridan's men resisted the most, but even they gave way and tried to join the end of Negley's division where the river bent north.

The river, shallow as it was, acted like a barrier in front of that end of the line, across which the Confederates would have to come, and the Pike, behind our lines, gave us the escape route we might need to get back to Nashville. As I rode around my men and positioned them at the far right to keep our troops from being outflanked, I could understand Thomas' thinking. He was giving his soldiers the best chance they could have in the worst of circumstances. And he was everywhere along the line, paying particular attention to the placement of his batteries above and behind the infantry and cavalry. It was no surprise to me that he paid such attention to his cannons: his training at West Point was in artillery, and he had proved himself in the Mexican War.

But once he had placed those guns, he got down off Ashes, his majestic horse, and stood in the midst of the privates doing the fighting, directing and supervising them along with their own officers. Wherever the fighting was thickest that day, Negley and Rousseau saw him, all of us did. Coolly giving orders in his dress uniform, he even told his men to lie down to steady their aim, then refused to lie down himself. The shot, shell, and canister came thick as hail, hissing, exploding, and tearing up the ground around us. You had no way of knowing where the next shell was going to land. But Thomas continued to walk up and down the line, watching the approaching enemy. I heard him say, distinctly, when the men begged him to get down, "No, it is my time to stand guard now."

Until that day, his men told me later, he was considered unnecessarily strict about the enforcement of orders, and was not especially liked. But on December 31, 1862, at Stone River, he captured an entire corps of men, his own, every one of whom would die for him from then on. It was a remarkable sight, because we were losing the battle after all. But that line he formed never broke as wave after wave of Hardee's and Polk's rebel troops poured across the field toward us, up the gradual incline from the river. Thomas just stood there in his new uniform with his newly minted brigadier general's stars and gold braid. He wanted to make certain that every man in the corps knew he was in the forefront, sharing their danger, and the full-dress uniform was a reminder they could not miss. Most generals save those uniforms for dances and ceremonies; Thomas used it for his men.

The roar of guns sounded like the pounding of a thousand anvils. Even that cannot explain the noise, because anvils are familiar. The sound of a battle of this magnitude is like nothing else. It is not constant, every moment is not like the last. The explosions and gunfire may come in waves but they are not regular waves. When it is loudest, you can see enemy soldiers, coming across the cotton fields, stuffing the cotton they have picked on the run into their ears. Absolutely everything is unpredictable, and most of all who is going to be hit or killed with the next sounds. You throw all fate to the winds because it is the only thing to do. And there is no point in running—Old Thomas will disapprove.

We did not retreat because there did not seem to be anywhere to go. With the Nashville Pike not a hundred yards behind us, it might as well have been five miles. The cloud of noise and smoke and flying men enveloped everything; none of us thought there was any place else to be. And the cedar thickets that concealed most of our infantry made us feel even more enclosed.

Finally, after a five-minute lull in the fighting late in the afternoon, General Thomas ordered, of all things, a bayonet charge! He rode up and down the line getting the men ready, and it was clear that they would go forward out of those woods, as long as the general said it was the thing to do. The remainder of Hardee's divisions, stalled in the middle of the long field down to the river, were completely startled by the charge and gave ground for a half mile to the base of the slope and their own cedar thickets.

We never regained our original positions from the morning. But we had the last word that day, and it proved to be prophetic. The Army of the Cumberland formed a new defensive line, still parallel with the railroad and pike, collected its wounded, and buried its heads in weariness behind breastworks thrown up in darkness.

That night there was a generals' council at Rosecrans' headquarters. We all heard that Thomas intensely disliked councils of war; he believed generals should be left to their own courage and ingenuity. All they needed to know was where everyone else was supposed to be. "Too much talking weakens the resolve of any army," he said. I learned only later that most of the generals were counseling retreat since we had lost so much ground. Thomas, with an assist from Sheridan, was roused from a catnap and stated his case clearly: "This army does not retreat," and that was the end of the meeting. He was forty-six but looked at least sixty that night, and no one, not even Rosecrans, was going to dispute his wisdom. The West Point Thomas was like a grandfather among the younger officers, so many of whom owed their rank to political appointments.

Forty thousand of our men, many in their first battle, lie stretched beside their guns on the field. The night is cold and gloomy, but our spirits, unaccountably, are rising. We all glory in the stubbornness with which Rosecrans, with Thomas in charge, has clung to our position. Once my horse has been tethered and settled down with the rest of our animals, I take out my pocket Bible and turn quite by accident to the 91st Psalm: "I will say to the Lord, He is my refuge and my fortress, my God: in Him will I trust. Surely He shall deliver thee from the share of the fowler, and from the noisome pestilence.... Thou shalt not be afraid for the terror by night; nor for the arrow that flieth by day;... A thousand shall fall by thy side, and ten thousand at thy right hand; but it shall not come nigh thee." Countless campfires glimmer. A few scattered shots are heard, and an occasional mounted man gallops by. But our spirits are lifting, and I wrap myself in my blanket and lie down for the night.

❖❖❖

Neither army wanted to fight the next day, but we knew it would come; neither was content with the first day's battle.

As I rode by an Ohio regiment in Rousseau's division the next morning, a gallant colonel gathered his field of men together and addressed them in an unusual way. I thought afterwards that his strange, cruel speech was true to what was likely to happen, even if we won the battle the following day:

> "Soldiers of the Third: The assault of the enemy on our fortifications will be made tomorrow morning. They will have twenty thousand men and forty cannon, more men and cannon than we have in this spot. They will cut us to pieces. Many of you will go into battle and never come back again. Marching into such an attack will be like marching to a butcher shop rather than to a battle."

The colonel spoke for another ten minutes in this same vein, and I took him aside when he finished and suggested, respectfully, that he might be upsetting the men for the battle that was coming. He only replied, "What I said was true, and they should know the truth."

Plutarch never included such a speech in his wars; his generals always spoke encouragingly and hopefully. But this colonel was his own person; maybe he wanted his men just to think of what was at stake. His men and I, as we listened, undoubtedly thought of what it would be like to die so young, so far from home. Of parents and family and sweethearts. Of things not said, and advice not heeded. Of the meaning of life itself, especially if, like I was, we were unsure of that meaning. Some soldiers, even before I moved away to my own men, kicked together the expiring fragments of their campfires, and when they raised their heads I could see how white their faces had become. Yes, the colonel revealed what we were fighting for and, for some of us, losing.

The sun rises on January 2nd and the Rebel cannon shells immediately begin falling along the Pike, like the wooden balls on those new bowling alleys bouncing toward the pins, but destroying them in the process. We rouse quickly, stuff our mouths, and mount to take the position, again on the right, that Thomas has assigned to me even before the sun rose. As I swing my horse around, a soldier near me, walking deliberately to the rear for safety, is struck by one of the cannon balls and separates in two, both halves—torso and head in one spot, and legs still together in another—still trying to move in that same direction, as if it is important any more. Our own batteries, thank goodness, immediately open up and silence the cannon fire coming in. The lull lasts till early afternoon.

Then from the left, where Van Cleve's regiment is located, comes the relentless sound of all guns, and all regiments, mounted or not, rush toward the center to bolster his men. The thunderous noise becomes more and more violent, the volleys of musketry growing into one prolonged and unceasing roll.

During the night, Van Cleve's men have moved forward and occupied a hill that the Rebels think is still unoccupied and ready for them to take, giving them a perfect base from which to conduct their real attack. And Thomas has repositioned his cannon to fire on the fields below Van Cleve's men, as if he knew the Confederates would want that hill. They ignored it two days before, but somehow Thomas knows they want it now. All tolled, fifty-eight guns decimate the half mile of space in front of our troops. And Negley's and Rousseau's divisions, on the defensive New Year's Eve, now rush across the river on the offensive to support Van Cleve. My men are held back. The battle lasts only two hours. The Rebels withdraw completely.

Our hungry soldiers cut steaks from the flanks of dead horses, and around the campfires talk over the incidents of the day. This is the most cheerful they have been since my regiment arrived, and they even give us a snatch of song now and then. Officers come over from adjoining brigades, hoping to find a little whiskey, only to discover the canteens empty long since, as are the private flasks.

I ride over the battlefield. The bodies of Federals and Confederates are intermingled everywhere, old and young, for miles. Some are my own men, one third of whom are missing. I see Corporal Wright lying at the exit from the cedar thickets when we first glimpsed the enemy two days before; he has one foot off and has bled to death. Another lies with his hands clasped behind his head, as if he is dreaming of home, but he is dead, too. The Confederates have the very same expressions on their faces as the Union dead: wherever they have gone they are presenting themselves to God in the same way.

A young boy, dressed in a Confederate uniform, lies face upward, eyes closed; there is no sign of a wound, and he looks as if he might be sleeping. I get down from my horse, and moving his rifle away from him, jostle his leg. I cannot believe he does not wake up, and I keep trying for what seems like minutes. A mule with one of his legs blown off has obviously been standing on three legs all day long; where could his strength be coming from, waiting for who knows what? How many poor men moaned through the cold night in the thick woods after that first day's battle, calling in vain for help, and finally dealing with God on their own.

❧❧❧

I find my men, back at camp, talking in hushed voices about comrades that have not returned. They assume they are dead, though some undoubtedly have fled. There are no laughs, not even the laughter of fear that comes with sorrow. A frivolous word would insult the slain. They have sought for a long time a grand battle, and have finally gotten one. They see it is like a storm through autumn leaves, and are amazed to discover that they are still attached to the tree.

Winter Quarters in Camp

I ask for volunteers to bring shovels to our position on the great battlefield. I have more volunteers than I have shovels. The men dig trenches for many bodies at once, most of which are stiff not from the cold but from rigor mortis. The only sound beside the shovels cracking the frozen dirt is the sobs from the volunteers, as they deposit their comrades in mass graves. The lines of General Wolfe at Quebec recur to me:

> No useless coffin enclosed his breast;
> Not in sheet or in shroud we wound him,
> But he lay like a warrior taking his rest,
> With his martial cloak around him.
>
> Slowly and sadly we laid him down
> From the field of his fame fresh and gory;
> We carved not a line, we raised not a stone,
> But left him alone with his glory.

As we are finishing, General Thomas rides into the middle of the field and stops. He looks at every soldier digging and, it seems, at every soldier being lowered in the ground. This time I am fifty yards away and cannot see his expression.

He does not move for ten minutes. Then he looks straight at me, salutes, and carefully, slowly, rides away.

Twelve hours later he led his thirty thousand remaining soldiers into Murfreesboro. His commander, General Rosecrans, rode next to him, but we all knew that Thomas was the reason we had taken the town. He was the backbone that refused to break, that gave us the courage we had needed. As he approached the city limits, he passed a little tumbled-down frame schoolhouse. Over the door, in large letters, were the words CENTRAL ACADEMY. I heard that Thomas said, "If this is called an academy, what sort of things must their common schoolhouses be? Tennessee is a beautiful state. All it lacks is free schools and free men."

The Negroes in the town may not have been free, but they poured out to greet us in great numbers, some of them in holiday attire. The women had flounces and the men had canes. One excited colored man told the truth about the two armies that had just tried to devastate each other: "You look like solgers. No wonder dat you wip de white trash ob de Southern army. Dey ced dey could wip two ob you, but I guess one ob you could wip two ob dem."

The six thousand white residents were nearly gone. The public square was deserted except for a few businesses that the quartermaster had commandeered. The wide, rutted streets were quiet.

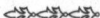

A week after we had settled into the town on every square of grass and in every abandoned and stately home, I rode back over the battlefield. Trees were peppered with buckshot, and some even cut down at the trunk. Unexploded shells threatened to trip me, and haversacks, hats, shoes, and broken caissons littered the fields. The grass in town was filled with moving, human life; but the grass at the river was filled with stillness and silent objects of all kinds. On the mounds of mass graves like the ones my men had made, wooden sticks, a foot apart, stood for each body beneath. The mounds and sticks were everywhere: in the woods, meadows, cornfield, cotton fields.

I even stumbled over a mound and its handful of sticks in

the deepest cedar thicket, where I had retreated to get away from the sight of the mounds in the open. On one of the sticks hung an old hat, still trying to protect the head of the soldier beneath. When spring comes the sticks will be gone and weeds will be up; by summer it will be impossible to find the shallower graves altogether.

3

After two weeks in Murfreesboro, always with the aroma of the corpses of horses from the battlefield in the air, we moved out, south toward Chattanooga. But it was slow going every day; neither Rosecrans nor Thomas seemed to want to chase the Rebels down, and boredom and desertion set in. When they drum a deserter out of the army, he is marched the length of the brigade to marshal music at the point of a bayonet. His head is shaved and sometimes a letter "D" is branded on his cheek. After all these changes, you would not have known that the momentum in the West was with us.

The Tennessee backcountry was exceedingly dusty and the only water was in the ponds. But in all of these the Confederates had dumped dead horses, mules, and dogs, to ruin the water for our use. We used the water anyway for our coffee, which had a strange soupy taste. Not surprisingly, our appetites suffered.

Almost every house along the road was deserted by men and occupied by either white women or Negro slaves. The few

Union men who still remained in southern Tennessee had, for weeks past, been hiding away in the hills, and since Stone River the secessionists were up there, too. We found a man on our fifth day out of Murfreesboro with his head cut off and his entrails ripped out, probably a Union man who had been hounded down by southern sympathizers who were being hounded themselves. "It was him or us," they'd say.

Daily routines never changed now. There was no sign of a coming battle, in which one army might finally crush the other. But Thomas would push us, demanding again and again that we do it right in drill so we could do it right in battle. Reveille at five in the morning, breakfast at six, surgeon's call at seven, drill, eight, recall, eleven, dinner, twelve, drill again at four, recall, five, guard mounting, five-thirty, first call for dress parade, six, second call, six-thirty, tattoo, nine, taps, nine-thirty. Every day like the last, even when we moved a few miles closer to Chattanooga.

Just now, one of my men lifts up his voice: "Someone is weeping for gallant Andy Gay, Who in death lies sleeping on the field of Monterey." Oblivious to the rain and the mud and the monotony of camp life, my thoughts drift to other scenes, when all I wanted was to be as safe as the farm families working the land back in Vernon.

The night sky clears and fills with stars and a rising moon. A thousand white tents dotting the roadside, the shadowy forms of soldiers. Another song: "The noise of the battle is over; the bugle no more calls to arms; a soldier no more, but a lover, I kneel to the power of thy charms. Sweet lady, dear lady, I'm thine."

I cannot help but think of Neala.

After that first big battle, all I could be sure about General

Thomas was that he was a quiet but steady commander. He noticed everything and planned for anything. When he gathered his troops together on the first day at Stone River, and my men helped them stop the stampede of infantry to the Nashville Pike and Chattanooga railway, they instantly believed in him, or at least in his ability to hold the line against bad odds.

My own cavalry, when he did not send them forward on that second day of fighting, were begging me to go to him and plead their case. They wanted to be trusted by him, too. I did not go. I did not know him well enough. But I could see even in my own men the effect he was beginning to have on the whole army. It was a feeling of being able to handle whatever came to them.

Not of winning always—no soldier by then thought that. Not even of not losing, though they would rely on him for that again and again.

It was a feeling of being ready.

His wife, Frances, gave me a letter years later that he wrote to her after Stone River. "Being ready" to him meant something beside winning.

My dear Frances,

We have had our first great engagement, and I will never know if it was worth it. You have read already, I am sure, about the battle near Murfreesboro, Tennessee, that the soldiers call "Stone River." I am alive, as are most of my men; as far as I can tell, the South lost more of its boys than we lost of ours. General Bragg did not serve his boys well, I am afraid. Some of them surely were from my home county in Virginia, just as some of ours were surely from Albany and your hometown. I prepare them to the best of my ability. I go out and watch my men bury their own and I no longer know what victory is. Is it measured by how many men are buried each time? Is it enough to measure it by who has moved a half mile toward the enemy's lines from the night before?

When I went to West Point, I assumed that becoming an officer at our nation's military college would give me a purpose and clarity. When events confronted me with a choice between serving the North or Virginia, that choice was clear. And I do not regret my decision. But now all I care about is planning a battle, any battle, to win with the fewest casualties. I will not let them say of me that, coming from the South, I made less than a total effort for the Union.

My hope is that some day my family will understand and forgive me. I miss you terribly, my dear Frances. Your support and affection are what sustains me.

Your loving George

It was nine months before we fought another big battle, at Chickamauga. The routine of camp life was relieved by a skirmish now and then, but very little was happening. Desertion was rampant, and generals' wives practically lived with their husbands. But General Thomas never took a leave during this time, and his wife never came from the East to pretend with him that there was not a war going on.

You would think that nine months would be enough time to devise a strategy to defeat the Rebels. We won a victory of sorts at Stone River and caused the Confederates to give up their first push to the Ohio River. And Grant had Vicksburg bottled up for months.

Winning the war was the issue. But the plan seemed to

be nothing more than waiting and moving and hoping. This was what finally ended Rosecrans' career in the West. He seemed to think that we could invade the South and win just by attrition, by one small battle after another. He could not grasp the fact that the Rebel cavalry alone, with countless quick strikes, would ruin that plan by frustrating our army enough to make the public in the North too impatient with the war.

General Thomas had a different idea of winning: you had to crush the Confederate army in the West with a major victory, one so large that they would give up and go home. He did not believe, like Grant, that having more soldiers in the field would be enough; that you could wear the South down through numbers. Our men would have to be better prepared, better equipped, and better supplied as well. And the weakest part of our army—the cavalry— had to be brought up to a level with the infantry and artillery. As long as Rosecrans was in charge, Thomas could prepare the army—and did for those nine months. But he could not pick his battles until he was the commander. At Chickamauga, the most violent two days of the entire war, he would have to make up for not being the commander by saving the army that Rosecrans, by his strategy of attrition, had left completely exposed in the northern Georgia thickets.

From January to September, we sat in camp or moved a few miles, inching our way toward the railroad center of Chattanooga. We guessed that General Bragg, commanding the Rebel forces, would make his stand at that city, with his troops and guns perched on the mountains surrounding Chattanooga, to rake us as we approached. Believing that may have made us more hesitant to proceed: when we all got there, Bragg would have the advantage.

I think the hesitancy that we all felt was what brought me into Thomas' confidence.

One night, after a few miles of marching in a steady rain, the boys go into camp hungry, wet, and tired, but soon enough have a hundred fires kindled and are eating their supper. Some fervent spirit, determined that the weather is not going to get him down, strikes up the national anthem:

> O! say, can you see by the dawn's early light,
> What so proudly we hailed at the twilight's last gleaming.

A hundred voices join in, and the distant mountains seem to resound with their own song:

> Whose broad stripes and bright stars, through the perilous fight, O'er the ramparts we watched were so gallantly streaming.

A band far off to the right is mingling its music with the voices, along with the occasional whinny of horses and squawk of mules in camp. I have ridden to Thomas' tent to deliver a routine report on the position of my troops for the night, and to get from him the orders for the morning.

I must have jumped back when I saw his eyes glistening, out of sight of the singing soldiers a few yards away. He said nothing as long as they continued through song after song, some patriotic, some romantic, some downright rude.

Without saying anything, he motioned for me to close the flap of the tent and sit down on the cot opposite him.

When the sounds diminished, he turned to me and began talking urgently in his Virginia drawl, "We've had time on our hands, William. I need to tell you that I have overheard some of our soldiers questioning why I am fighting for the North. As much as I understand their confusion, their words still sting. But when I am with you I feel a kinship, so I suspect I can talk to you, and I need to speak with someone. Can I trust you with my thoughts, Colonel Swain? I cannot trust anyone above me in command, and I would not share my feelings with any of my generals. We all need to appear strong, all of the time."

"General Thomas, I am honored that you would consider me a trustworthy person, and I can assure you that anything you tell me will remain confidential."

"Thank you, William.... You know, in the South the army determines public opinion and is unaffected by it. Everyone hopes for their victories and hangs on the latest news. I am a Southerner. I know. But in the North the army has no effect on public sentiment, yet we are slaves to it nevertheless. Our people clamor for action—and force us to move too soon, as at Fredericksburg and Bull Run. They have to be patient; we have to push deliberately, but patiently. We should consolidate regiments, and send home thousands of politically appointed officers who take their pay and give us nothing in return. More will die if we just keep fighting one inconclusive battle after another with no plan on either side.

"General Lee pleaded with me to join him and fight for Virginia before I made my decision." The General paused. "I had fought with him in Texas, and we were the best of friends then and still were in eighteen sixty-one. He told me that no one in Washington had a right to tell us in Virginia how to live our lives; if we wanted to have slaves, that was our business. We contributed to the economy of the nation. We were not forcing slaves on anyone else. We were the ones who set the highest tone for public service in this country. The great politicians in our history had come from Virginia, not Boston and New York, and many of them, like Jefferson, had slaves. It did not keep them from thinking great thoughts and inspiring the North as well as the South."

The songs outside had started up again, in the distance. He continued, deliberately and intently, looking right at me.

"But I was not swayed by Lee's argument—amazingly, I was not. I could not have admired or liked a man more than I admired and liked Robert E. Lee. I think he expected that I would be moved by what he had said. Not only was I not affected by what he said, I came away from his speech believing less in the cause of the South than ever before. I simply said to him, 'Robert, this is going to be a horrible war. It will not just divide and destroy families. It will threaten the existence of the country itself, not only the government in Washington. When that break up starts it will never stop. The South will not hold together. It will begin to shatter into smaller and smaller units—states, counties, municipalities, towns. All that holds the South together is its rural life and slavery, two things that you cannot build a lasting culture on. Take away the North and you do not even have the cotton mills that process the raw material that slaves pick.

"I told him I had to fight for the North because I could not conceive of what America would look like otherwise. I am not an abolitionist, William, but when I was young I chose to teach slaves on our plantation to read; even if they were not citizens and might never be, I believed they still deserved to read and write. My father, a gracious and dignified man, disagreed but did not interfere with my belief in their right to literacy. He set me on this road of independent thinking.

"I told Robert E. Lee that I would fight for the Union because there was no hope for any country within our borders— nothing that could be called America—if I did not. And if President

Lincoln ordered the abolition of slavery, I told him, I would not feel a moment of grief. You talk about what Virginia has given this country. Beside our founding documents, Virginia has given us hundreds of thousands of darkened minds that are beginning to catch glimpses of the sun of a better life now rising before them.

"This time Lee was silent. He walked past me, without expression, and I have not set eyes on him since."

His speech was guarded and emotional at the same time.

"I lost my great friend that day, William. I lost my family, too. I wired them with my decision from New York City, but they never responded, and I will never talk to them again. People in the South are polite only up to a point; if you threaten what they hold most dear, the system that enables them to live well, you have done something worse than murder. It is an act of disloyalty that is beyond indecency. My parents were already dead, thank goodness, but people I still communicate with in Southampton Country have told me that my sisters have turned all my pictures to the wall and refuse to speak my name...

There was a long pause, a deep breath.

Then, suddenly composed, he took my hand and thanked me.

4

few minutes later, as I walked unsteadily to my horse in the drizzle that had started up again, all I could think of was an old hymn I learned back home, one the free Negroes of Vernon knew as well as I did and sang just as often:

> There is a land of pure delight,
> Where saints immortal reign;
> Infinite day excludes the night,
> And pleasures banish pain.
>
> There everlasting spring abides,
> And never withering flowers;
> Death, like a narrow sea, divides
> This heavenly land from ours.

General Thomas was going to deal out death to get the rest of us, somehow, closer to that land where day excludes the night. I knew at that moment that he himself would have stayed behind in that "narrow sea," if that is what it took.

38

By the time I had gotten back to my own men two miles away, I thought I understood a more personal reason that General Thomas chose to fight for the North over the South: he wanted to protect his boys even as he sent them into battle, and in some strange way, like the most responsible parent, the more boys he could watch over—South as well as North—the more lives he could try to salvage, the better he would have done his job.

Riding back to my men, I could not avoid my own reasons for going to war.

My father hated me and I could never please him. As his only child, I was the target of his drunken rage. My mother died when I was twelve years old, and I have always believed she left this world to escape from him.

Everything I did was ridiculed—from my choice of profession to joining the army. After a year of reporting about the war in my newspaper, I suddenly realized that Confederate troops could march into southern Indiana very easily. One reason was Shiloh, a battle the past spring in Tennessee. Our troops luckily won by reinforcements arriving in time for the second day. Until then, all the major battles had been in the East. People forget that state's rights cut two ways in the war—the North did not want Southerners on our soil any more than they wanted us on theirs. That was what decided the most famous battle of the war—Gettysburg—it was fought on Northern soil, in Pennsylvania, north of Washington, DC!

"You're a fool to put your life on the line for a bunch of niggers," my father shouted at me. "You've always been an idealist, and that's another word for a damned jackass." His eyes were alive with anger. When I tried to explain my position, he just insulted me further. "And that woman you're courting is nothing but an Irish whore. I didn't raise you to fill your house with a bunch of mic kids and that's what she'll do."

Here I was preparing to risk my life for what I believed was a just cause, and his response was to attack me and my beloved Neala. Even then, I could not find the courage to confront him. My mother taught me to be silent in the hope that he would fall into a stupor and sleep it off. Now I did that automatically. I was so ashamed of my cowardice.

The following day I had a final delivery for my father to Neala's father's farm before reporting for duty. Helping him with his farm equipment business was my way of pacifying him, and keeping him from pestering me about joining him after the war. He could not wait to add "and Son" to his public notices in the county. It seemed the only way he would acknowledge me, and I wanted no part of it.

The Monaghan horse farm was the talk of Vernon. Liam Monaghan and his three children had arrived from Kentucky in 1861 after his son John had been killed at Manassas fighting for the Rebs. Mr. Monaghan brought his slaves with him and freed them when they arrived. All but one stayed and worked his thoroughbreds for show and sale. "I taught them everything I know," he said in his lilting brogue.

"John and I had a parting of the ways about slavery. He was a true believer in the Southern way of life, having been born there and all. I hope God will forgive me for using human beings in that way, but I never would have been successful without them. They deserve whatever we can give them after what we put them through."

His honesty was disarming... ever the critic of my news-paper articles, but praising when he felt it was warranted. A quick wit and fiercely loyal, yet melancholy and blunt as hell. I am told that is an accurate description of the Irish, and I liked and admired him very much.

And then there was Neala. Our first encounter was memorable.

Imagine a small but fierce tornado coming at you, Neala on her thoroughbred—chestnut in color, matching the hair of its rider. It was as if she and that stallion of hers were one, their movement fluid and graceful. I knew from Liam that its foundation was Arabian, and he was a spectacularly handsome and intelligent companion.

Neala and I sparred with each other. It was clear there was an attraction but I feared I was no match for her. She took my breath away.

"So you're a newspaper man." Her accent was pure Kentucky. And being the too-serious chap that I was, I responded with "Yes, but I am considering going to war at the moment." I felt pathetic next to her.

She came right back: "Civil war is anarchy, not civility. Our democracy is in its infancy and it is already challenged. Over what? Profit and gentility? Can you see the hypocrisy, Colonel Swain? Civility hides the real truth: greed."

I was completely captured.

She must have resembled her mother, who had died several years before, her beauty embodied in this dark creature with her black eyes and full features. I wondered if her mother were as opinionated and forthright as she. Neala had been cherished. She knew who she was.

Much to my surprise, she offered to correspond with me, as she did with others, if I joined this atrocious war. She felt it was her duty as a citizen and a woman who could not fight herself.

"The Negroes deserve their freedom," she said. "I'll ignore the warmongers and profiteers and concentrate on those who are making the greatest sacrifice of all. I hope they believe it's worth it."

"Your interest in all our soldiers is appreciated, Neala," I told her. "I will try not to bore you with my musings."

"You will not bore me, William. It will give us a chance to become better acquainted. I do find you interesting, if a bit shy."

She finds me interesting! My hope that we could be more than friends was renewed after such a harsh start.

She offered me her hand and wished me good luck. I felt like I could conquer the world.

❖❖❖

One Sunday edition, several months earlier, I had finally taken matters into my own hands, after wiring the governor and, with the banker James Lanier's help, getting his approval and a colonel's commission:

EXPERIENCED CAVALRY AND RIDERS WANTED
NEW INDIANA REGIMENT FORMING IN VERNON
Wire Colonel William Swain
Assemble on the Vernon Green at Noon 1 Week from Today

My paper reached the entire county, and I knew that there were enough farm boys out there with riding experience to make up a regiment of four hundred soldiers. We might not have the right horses and equipment, but I had a week to work with the governor to find out how and where we were going to get them.

The real question was whether each soldier could arrange for the farm to be taken care of when he went off to war. I was confident I could inspire them if they showed up on the Vernon Green. But they would still have to convince their families that it was the right thing to do.

It was a crowd of all ages. They filled the side streets off the corners of the Green; by twelve-thirty, there was no room for the riders to dismount. All I could do was roll up a newspaper like a megaphone, and deliver my patriotic speech as I turned in all four directions on the bandstand at the center of the Green—and hope that the men on the outskirts could hear me.

I think they came to be persuaded, to be shown that there was something more heroic for them than the farm life they knew. The war was a horrible experience for everyone, a civil war tearing the country apart. There was hardly a family in the North that did not have doubts about the Northern cause, or the official reasons for fighting. Just the idea of fighting against your own countrymen, when everyone knew that the economy of the North and the country's whole political system was dependent on the South, made no sense to many people above the Ohio River. If the South had not tried to expand slavery into Texas in the Mexican War and Kansas after that, I think the rest of the country would have left them alone.

One thing was clear in my mind: most of those recruits that Sunday afternoon could not, like Governor Morton himself, care a whit about whether slavery existed or not below the Ohio or east of the Mississippi. They did not care whether Negroes could vote. Negroes were invisible to them—just cogs in the wheel that was controlled by white men in the South and North.

No, I think their reason for joining my regiment was that they could not imagine themselves without a country. It was the shame of it, maybe—losing what the last war in the last century had stood for and achieved. And that was the reason I shouted to them that day on the green.

5

We expected the Rebels to defend Chattanooga to the teeth, with their artillery placed on the mountains surrounding the city. This was the railway hub of the West. So we dropped into Alabama and Georgia behind the city to encircle it and come at Bragg from all directions.

But the Rebels abandoned the city on their own, a few days before we arrived. And General Rosecrans made the first of his many mistakes in September 1863: he thought they left because they were afraid of his army. General Bragg was taking a big chance in letting Union forces occupy Chattanooga, but his gamble paid off. Rosecrans spread our troops into three massive columns, miles apart, and pushed into Georgia hoping to destroy the weak Rebel army with whichever column encountered them. That is how little respect he had for the enemy, and it cost him his command and nearly his entire army. When General Thomas halted his column where Rosecrans directed, on the other side of the mountains around Chattanooga, next to Chickamauga Creek in Georgia, we became the ones pursued.

The War in Tennessee

What followed was the most violent battle of the war, two days of complete chaos. At the end of the second day, the outcome hinged completely on the character of a single general, George Henry Thomas.

❦❦❦

General Rosecrans had done a fine job of pushing Bragg deeper into the South, but it had been without much action or loss of life. You would think that was a good thing; I even remember Thomas dutifully complimenting Rosecrans on his success without any significant battles. But in his deeper moments Thomas would speak to me about the need for a massive battle to decide a war; sooner or later, one army was going to have to defeat the other completely. It might not be one large battle; maybe it would be two or three large ones. But it could not be done by pushing an army around without conflict or by waiting for the politicians in Washington to settle things. We were in too far for that. Thomas was right, it would take a conflagration, and he knew that Rosecrans was not the man for that kind of war. He admired him for his abilities, and always remained loyal to a fault, but he was certain that Rosecrans could not produce a plan for ending what had been started.

By the morning of September 19th, the day I have already told you about, everyone in both armies knew some things about each other and were ignorant about other things. Rosecrans had realized a few days before that Bragg was not running from him toward Atlanta, but had turned near Lafayette, Georgia to fight. So Rosecrans was furiously trying to get his three columns together that he had spread over sixty miles on the other side of Chattanooga. It would take days for Crittenden's and McCook's men to reach Thomas, who seemed to be in front of the Rebel force; but by the 19th Crittenden's men had arrived after a long forty-mile forced march, and McCook's were just a few miles away. If Bragg had attacked a few days earlier, I do not think it would have mattered how much character and will General Thomas had. He would have been completely outnumbered right from the start. Now, on the 19th, there was a chance, even if our backs were to the mountains south of the city.

What the two sides could not have known about each other was exactly where they were. That area of Georgia, where it is not mountainous, is full of thickets with very few open fields. Even when you find some height from which to gaze over a distance, you cannot see anything: there are too many notches and gaps and it is much too overgrown to have any idea of how big or where the opposing forces really are. You can feel them for sure. You know they are right there. But are they two miles down the road one way or the other, or right in front of you? We still did not realize how large Bragg's army had gotten, with reinforcements from the losses at Vicksburg and Gettysburg. If we had, we would have known that the enemy was two miles down the road to our left, two miles down the road to our right, and right in front of us! The rain and fog made the uncertainty even worse.

This was the battle Thomas had been waiting for. But it was not going to be fought on his terms or according to any plan he would have approved.

My regiment of cavalry were among the few mounted soldiers he had, and he did not dare spare us to scout out the enemy. Since there were so few fields amidst the cedar thickets in this wilderness, our movements would be slowed too much and we would be too vulnerable to snipers. So he kept us close to the end of the battle line that seemed most likely to be attacked. Cavalry is especially good at keeping the enemy from turning your flank; we can flare out and move quicker than infantry to prevent the enemy's infantry from swinging around the end. Of course we might meet the enemy's own cavalry and often did. Most of our mounted fights happened when we encountered the enemy trying to use its cavalry in the same way. So Thomas assumed he would need us on the flank that was most vulnerable. The trouble was, we did not know which end that would be, to the north nearer Chattanooga, or to the south where McCook was still trying to get in line.

That morning, after trying to sleep above the mud on three wooden rails, I was at Thomas' headquarters in the old Kelly House before dawn to learn where he guessed we would be needed. As I rode up, I could not believe my eyes. I knew General Thomas had a sense of propriety, and that, big as he was, he loved to eat well.

But I did not expect what I saw only a few hours before a major battle was sure to begin: breakfast laid out on tables with white tablecloths, silver plate, crisp white napkins, silver water goblets, and china cups. The food, the smell of which I can still recall, was fresh smoked beef, ham, hot rolls and potatoes. Punch and black coffee in abundance were there to drink. As dawn crept in, the mountains loomed above us and the fog wound through the trees, but we ate as if we were sitting in Chattanooga's best restaurant. The general was there, tall and sedate, dressed in his best uniform. But how can I explain how unpretentious he remained—modest to a fault, intensely concerned about his men being protected by being in the best military positions for the fight to come.

As we ate, trying to plan what could not really be planned, I could see the campfires of our soldiers strike up all around us as they began their own breakfasts of hardtack, bacon, and coffee. The men were warming themselves by breaking up fences and making larger fires, ones the Rebels might see. But everyone now was so resigned to fate, to the fact of battle, that no one believed that large or small fires, seen by the enemy, would make a bit of difference in the hours that followed.

Sure enough, promptly at seven, an aide from General Brannan came riding furiously through the fires and into General Thomas' camp, shouting that Croxton's men were seriously engaged on the left—you could begin to hear the artillery—and that it was far more than a skirmish. He said every gap in the thickets showed a gray soldier moving toward Brannan's end of the line. General Thomas calmly turned to me and said, "You know what to do, Bill." And all of us sprang to our horses.

I looked back as I rode off, and the white tablecloths and silver goblets were still in their places. General Thomas was nowhere to be seen.

I have already described that first day at Chickamauga, when the cannonball sailed past Thomas' head as I tumbled off my own horse. One brigade after another on both sides of Chickamauga Creek hurled themselves into battle, beginning in the north with Croxton and falling south like dominoes until McCook's men were engaged at the end of the day. The bravery on both sides was remarkable, especially the volunteers, as mine were. (General Wood was supposed to have said, after Colonel King's regulars folded under a Rebel charge, "Between regulars and volunteers, I would choose volunteer troops. They don't know when they're whipped; they'll fight as long as they can pull a trigger.")

My men followed Croxton's mounted infantry that day and took the brunt of the early morning charge. I lost dozens of my farm boys. We never left that single square mile patch of ground for eight hours, I am proud to say. Sometimes we mounted; sometimes we stayed low. When dark came, I was standing next to the body of our color bearer who had been shot down in his tracks at eight in the morning, his flag falling against my own horse. We were still in our positions.

By nightfall, the Rebels were on our side of Chickamauga Creek and had gained perhaps three hundred yards, and we were tightening our line another two hundred yards further back. I think Rosecrans decided to make a stand right there, neither retreating through McFarland's Gap nor preparing to attack. The enemy had lost as many men as we; maybe we could at least wear him out, frustrate his plans, and discourage him into leaving. It was not likely. Both sides were squeezed into a three by six mile strip between the mountains and the creek, and were going to fight it out there.

A heaviness settled on all of our men the closer they moved together. Out in front of them, on the darkest, coldest night of the Fall, could be heard the moans and cries of thousands of fallen soldiers. You could not tell which side they were on—there is no Southern accent in moans. Litter bearers were working to exhaustion, but there was so little light—only a sliver of the moon—and the thickets were so dense that the only soldiers they reached were the ones lucky enough to fall in the open.

Toward morning, they brought in an Ohio soldier whose head wound had frozen his face to the ground. He died soon after.

No fires were allowed. When some Tennessee soldiers lit a circle of cigarettes, they were struck with a dozen rounds of shot. It did not take much; the enemy was right there, in the pitch dark. Put freezing soldiers in a wood so dense that you cannot see the stars, with no certainty of where your regiment ends and the enemy begins, and add the intense thirst of having no other creeks to drink from to soothe our parched throats, and you understand the night of September 19th and the morning of September 20th. No one slept.

During the night, my cavalry managed to go eight miles south of our position and fill a thousand canteens with spring water. We tried to distribute them throughout the three corps, but it barely made a difference. Fifty thousand divided by one thousand means a canteen for every fifty soldiers. And that is not counting the wounded, who came first.

At midnight, Rosecrans had called his commanders together, and General Thomas held them firm again, the way he did at Stone River after the first day's fight. He even wanted, he told me later, to tighten up McCook's divisions from the south and turn them perpendicular to his own and Crittenden's on the spurs of Missionary Ridge overlooking Dry Valley Road. Rosecrans overruled him, but that is exactly where the remnants of those same divisions ended up the next day when they were routed by Longstreet.

Both days at Chickamauga were fought on instinct. Or rather, the generals who were successful—like Longstreet and Thomas—seemed to have an abundance of that quality. There was no way the terrain and the weather would allow for anything resembling confidence and logic. You could see it all on Rosecrans' face when he and Thomas rode by the men at six a.m. on the 20th. His words were hopeful—"We shall whip them"—but his face was ashen, and he crossed himself repeatedly. Most of us were raised Protestant back home and had no particular use for Catholics like Rosecrans in our regular lives, but in battle, the last thing we wanted was our Catholic commander crossing himself as if his faith was wavering.

Thomas tried to be optimistic, too. "Whenever I touched the Rebels' flanks yesterday," he told Rosecrans, "they broke." We were all scared, even Thomas I think, and that did not bode well either.

We knew it was going to be worse than yesterday.

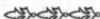

The second day was a duplicate of the first, with two big differences: there were twice as many charges, since more troops had arrived on both sides during the night, and Rosecrans created a gap in our line that the Rebels poured through. Without the second development, it might have been the decisive Union victory Thomas wanted. As it was, it was nearly the worst Union defeat of the war. Still, General Thomas was this battle, he was everywhere anything was happening, as if he anticipated everything except what it would take to win. And that was not his fault.

September 20th was a Sunday. The day was going to be warmer than the 19th, you could already tell as the dawn came. It was a light-struck autumn day in the lower Appalachians. There seemed to be fog in the air, but it was only the mist rising from Chickamauga Creek. It was perfectly quiet, a complete opposite to the noisy night spent chopping down trees and building breastworks to protect ourselves from the charges that were sure to come. The silence was ominous. Only the sound of pans and cups at breakfast broke the quiet.

Hours passed, soundlessly, with only the clopping of horses and the loading of guns to remind us of what we were about to do. Finally, the sound of artillery began on the far left of our line, just where the Confederates attacked the previous day. This was exactly what Thomas expected and where he had concentrated the log works and artillery during the night. I had been on the far left myself with my regiment on Saturday; now Thomas kept me close to his headquarters a mile to the south. This time he knew he had enough infantry. It was Breckenridge's Rebel division that attacked and had to be turned back by Beatty and Baird, and some of Johnson's, Palmer's, and Reynolds' brigades. The fighting was fierce, but every charge was thwarted because, like the previous day, the enemy came one brigade at a time. Breckenridge and Bishop Polk could never have seen the battle clearly if they had combined all their Rebel brigades, but they might have turned our left if they had done so. Just the delay in starting their attack till nine-thirty gave us time to prepare, since we knew from General Thomas that an attack was coming just where it did. Some of the gray-clads got to within thirty yards of the breastworks, but each time they charged they were driven back with fearfully decimated ranks. Two hours later, the fighting began to slide down the battle line, and the troops to the north resorted to long-range sniping till late in the afternoon.

The real battle came to the south, and again Brannan's brigade bore the brunt, as they had at the north end the day before.

It was Thomas' own aide, Sanford Kellogg, who created the very event that Thomas must have feared. As the fighting moved south, so did Kellogg to review the position of the divisions. To Reynolds' right was supposed to be Brannan, but he and his five thousand men could not be seen at all. Four hundred yards further down the road Wood's division of Crittenden's corps could be clearly seen on this side of the tree line. Kellogg panicked. He came racing back into camp with the news that Brannan's men had disappeared, that Reynolds' flank was completely exposed and the Rebels could charge right through. Thomas immediately sent him on to Rosecrans, a mile and a half away, for confirmation. Others were giving Rosecrans the same report: apparently there were no men between Reynolds and Wood. So Rosecrans fired off an order to General Wood to close up on Reynolds "and support him." No one asked Crittenden, Wood's commanding general, if Brannan was gone next to Wood, and no one asked Wood himself. The battle was clearly coming that way, and there didn't seem to be time for every step in the chain of command.

Rosecrans had just ridden up and down the lines himself and had seen nothing of the kind, yet he also panicked when the reports came in. A huge mistake had been made: there was no gap in the line! But when Rosecrans moved Wood's five thousand men to the left, he created one. The simple phrase in General Wood's order to "support" Reynolds he interpreted to mean "back up" Reynolds, because he—Wood—knew Brannan was there, in the forest, his men obscured from view, and so he thought the order meant to go behind Brannan and position his men behind Reynolds, "in support" of him.

The gap opened, and at the very moment that General

Longstreet, with his twenty-five thousand troops that had come by train from their bitter loss at Gettysburg, were set to attack Brannan and Wood!

Moments like this in battle, though they are like chaos on the ground, have to seem strangely coincidental when looked back upon. What are the chances that an entire division would disappear from sight, and their own commander would not be asked where they are? Or that another division would be moved to replace them from exactly the spot that the enemy was going to attack next? And one other fact. General Thomas on the left had been asking all night for more reinforcements from the divisions on the right, and General Negley's had been sent up to him. But Negley's division had not arrived by morning, and was still nowhere to be seen at nine-thirty when the battle started in the north and at eleven when the gap opened in the center. His five thousand men were wandering behind our lines toward Rossville, and never were available for Thomas, who got by without them, or at the broken center where Negley's men had been positioned right behind Wood, the division that had been moved!

Longstreet's divisions literally poured through the opening left by Wood, battered Connell"s brigade of Brannan's division as it turned to the south to fight them, and completely cut off the divisions of Davis and Sheridan on our right from the rest of our army. The men in those divisions just headed backwards in flight. There was so little resistance to Longstreet's troops that they ran the mile past the Brotherton farm to Widow Glenn's house, where Rosecrans had his headquarters. The general jumped on his horse and fled to the rear himself with his entire staff only minutes ahead of the Rebel charge. All through the rushing of troops and the collapsing of the dead and wounded, the four Brotherton cows never moved, munching grass, instinctively avoiding the bullets and cannonballs sailing around them. When the Brotherton family returned after the battle, their cows were there, with nine dead Union soldiers in their front yard.

Unlike the previous day, when neither side could gain a few hundred yards, in fifty minutes almost half the Rebel army had moved, against almost no resistance, two thousand yards around the right flank of what was left of our forces. Thomas had worried so much on the 19th about our left flank being turned; now, without his knowing it, our right flank had been. And his commanding general was heading through McFarland's Gap for Chattanooga and not turning back. Not only that, the other two corps commanders were with him, McCook and Crittenden, with Phil Sheridan not far behind.

Of course, Thomas did not know all that when he got the first report at his headquarters that a large mass of men were approaching from the south and had fired on our men; he asked for an explanation from the officers around him, including me, and got no answers. He made clear that we would have to return fire, but quickly sent me and a company of men to find out exactly what had happened to our right just as his own men were winning the battle on our left.

He no longer appeared nervous. He always looked immovable, like a mountain. But his countenance was even firmer than his size, the square jaw, with steady blue eyes dominating through bushy eyebrows, the ruddy complexion. He somehow could stand perfectly erect and seem relaxed. He never raised his voice except to yell occasionally above the sound of cannon fire.

Now, at the Kelly house, he just looked at me and said, "This is what I feared. Yesterday I moved to the left on the outside of Crittenden and we stopped them. If I had been in the center today, where Rosecrans always had me before, I could have seen the trouble coming and countered it. But it has found me anyway and I will have to respond. Colonel Swain, go quickly with your men and find out who it is that is threatening us and how bad it looks. We are still in danger on the left, so I will have to fight with different men on the right." Even without knowing that Rosecrans and the others were gone, he assumed he was going to be in charge.

There did not seem to be an ounce of vanity in his demeanor. The pain, however, was excruciating. It was as if his steely eyes looked right through me to the soldiers he imagined in flight from those oncoming men in gray. Falling like the leaves that were already dropping from the trees, thinking at that last minute of what they might have been if they were anywhere but lying on these strange, rugged fields. As the blood ebbs out of them, any thoughts of home, of the thousand and one scenes of their old life, must increase their shame of dying in flight.

This time as I mount up, I look back and he is standing in the front door. "When you find me again," he says, "I will have moved south. I want to see those boys, too, what I fear is left of them. God help them." He looks toward the increasing tremors from the south.

❧❧❧

It turns out I do not have far to go. We head west two hundred yards to turn left on the road to Widow Glenn's house where General Rosecrans is supposed to be. As I reach the crossroads and look down the road to the south, I can see the enemy running from side to side on the road less than half a mile away, much closer than Rosecrans' headquarters. The commander is either dead or captured or fled. There is no point in going south. We need to get to a height of some kind to see how many of the enemy are close.

So instead of turning left we keep riding straight through a line of trees, cathedral-like, with no undergrowth and the ground clean enough for a picnic, and emerge on the other side near the base of Snodgrass Hill. The hill is more like a series of humpbacks, mostly cleared of trees, rising a few hundred feet with only shallow ravines in between. None of our men were there in the morning but they are coming here now.

I ride toward them from behind, where the slope is more gradual. When I reach them I will also have the view I want of the plains between the hill and Lafayette Road. If the Rebels are pushing us back, I will see it clearly from there.

The first person I recognize is Colonel Hunter of Bloomington, the commander of Brannan's 82nd Indiana, with perhaps two hundred fifty of his men just reaching the top of the hill and firing back down into an enemy I cannot see. His men seem to know what to do, turning every fifty yards or so; Hunter ignores them and is chasing down soldiers from other regiments and trying to pull them into his own. He does not yet know I have come from General Thomas three-quarters of a mile away, but he yells to me anyway, as if he did not care who hears him, "I will not retreat another inch." He has fallen back at least a mile from his position in the morning.

I have halted my company fifty yards or so behind the line that Hunter is beginning to form on the crest, behind rocks and trees, and I ride through them to see what his men are shooting at. I do not yet know if they have a good reason to be here; at least they are still fighting, I tell myself.

Then I know. One look down the hill from the crest, across the fields of the Brotherton Farm to Lafayette Road and the dense woods beyond, and I understand. The entire right half of our army is gone! I do not mean they are not in sight. I mean that there are no lines, no clear groups of men, no formations, no one in blue near Lafayette Road. I see our men, thousands and thousands of them, but they are running to the right as fast as they can, some stopping quickly and firing, most not even looking back. I try to make out any commanders. These are not Thomas' brigades so I am not sure I can identify anyone from a distance. A few of their generals are trying to halt the stampede, waving their swords menacingly at the hatless heads of any soldiers around them.

Most of the running men are not coming toward Snodgrass Hill but seem to be circling it to the right on a direct line to McFarland's Gap two miles away and the road to Rossville and Chattanooga. Some mounted officers are calmly riding next to them.

But pockets of men, no larger than small regiments, are turning up the slope to the top of the hill. I cannot understand why they are turning and others are not, I cannot hear what is being said to them by their commanders on foot or mounted. And most do not turn. But the 9th Ohio and the 2nd Minnesota, both of Van Derveer's brigade, also from General Brannan's division, arrive at the top and join the 82nd Indiana at the most exposed point of the Hill. Moments later John Brannan himself rides up with his aide and hails me. He starts to ask me to take a message to Thomas, not realizing that I came for just that purpose.

But as my horse moves so I can hear him better, the smoke clears and I have a full view of the plains beyond our fleeing soldiers.

Brannan stops when he sees the shock on my face.

I cannot believe my eyes. Pushing beyond those running men in blue are not just the enemy. There have to be fifteen thousand gray clad soldiers in full view, in dress order, as far as the eye can see, marching relentlessly in a single direction. Ranks follow ranks in close order, moving steadily and briskly toward us. And the first rank cannot be more than a few hundred yards in front of the crest. Brannan himself turns to command the first few rounds fired at those men, and I wait, stunned, to hear how all this could have happened.

In all those days when I was writing accounts of battles for the *Vernon Banner*, I never once had occasion to describe a charge as monumental as this one. Even the stories I read before Chickamauga of Pickett's charge at Gettysburg could not compare. Not that there were less men at Gettysburg, not that. But there we waited for them, and outnumbered them when they arrived. Here they are pursuing our frightened soldiers, and Brannan's troops, fast assembling on Snodgrass Hill, cannot number more than a thousand men by my quick estimation. We do not even have a battery set up yet to enfilade the dense ranks of the oncoming Rebels. There is no hope at all.

I cannot wait for an explanation. Brannan is too busy and I know what I have to tell General Thomas. I wheel my horse, catch up my men as I fly back down the hill, and head east to the Kelly farm. As long as the Rebels have not penetrated the Glenn Road any further, I can get to Thomas in five minutes' ride.

I do not have to. He is coming out of the trees as I reach the base of the hill, his hat in hand slapping the flanks of his mount. He has heard the increasing gunfire and, as promised, has "moved south." I simply yell to him what I observed, and, without even halting his horse, he sweeps by me and I ride back up the hill in his train. He arrives at the front line just in time to see the 2nd Minnesota position itself next to Hunter. Even with bullets flying past his head, he smiles as members of his original brigade when the war began move calmly and purposefully into position, then fire off a round not more than thirty seconds later. I begin assembling my men behind them, after our horses are settled in the ravine nearby.

From that point on during the rest of September 20th,

1863, General Thomas is everywhere on Snodgrass Hill giving commands. Sometimes he rides right behind the assembling regiments, at other times he walks amidst them. When he has to confer with General Brannan or General Wood, whose men are also rising to the challenge and appearing from the east, Thomas rides back a few hundred yards to a clump of dead trees on the gradual downslope of the Hill. The longer the afternoon goes on, the harder it becomes to hear, and the more often he has to retreat for five minutes at a time to try to carry out a battle plan that will enable his strange mix of regiments from all over the battlefield to fight off troops that outnumber them at least four to one. He sits on his horse, listening to the awful fire that rages along the line, with the coolness of assured victory or the calmness of despair.

He is at the front line when they bring in General Lytle of McCook's division. His men were the only ones under Sheridan's command who have resisted the onslaught, and Lytle has fallen with three bullets in his spine. Still conscious, he does not speak but smiles gratefully at the officers and orderlies carrying him up the hill and over the crest. They lay him under the first tree behind the lines and he motions them back into action. He unfastens his sword and hands it to an orderly. And he dies quietly. I look down at him and remember the poet not the general, the most famous soldier poet we had in the north. I had to memorize his "Antony and Cleopatra" in school:

> I am dying, Egypt, dying,
> Ebbs the crimson life-tide fast....
> Let thine arm,
> Oh Queen, enfold me....

I printed it countless times in my newspaper. The South had its romantic leaders, we had William Lytle.

The soldiers from both sides are now so close together that they grab each other's uniforms, guns, flags, canteens, anything that can keep them from separating again. If a line of combatants falls back it is immediately replaced by another line from behind them. To get to us they are climbing, literally climbing, over the bodies of their fallen comrades. We have the advantage of position, they have the advantage of men.

The 21st Ohio, one of Negley's regiments that didn't wander off during the day, is armed with Colt repeating rifles. Most of our men have Enfields, single-shot guns that require reloading after every firing. When Longstreet's troops rise up in front of the 21st, they expect to have a chance to rush forward when our troops are reloading; but the second and third volleys catch them at once, and decimate their ranks. Even so, the 21st need every advantage—Hindman's Rebels come at them five times and have to be repulsed five times. The five hundred thirty-five soldiers of the 21st Ohio fire forty-three thousand rounds at the charging enemy. They even resort to jamming some Enfield rounds into their Colt rifles. From one o'clock in the afternoon when the Rebel charges up Snodgrass Hill begin, to sundown, the very earth trembles with musketry, and finally our artillery begins to make a difference as well. By our good luck, General Thomas and General Brannan are the two best artillerists in the army, and they both are on the crest of that hill on the 20th of September. One furious attack after another, and our men stay frozen to the hill, while the artillery mows smooth the ground in front.

The Battle of Chickamauga:
Thomas's Men Repelling the Charges of the Rebels

Midway through the battle we finally get some good luck, just as the gap created by Rosecrans at eleven was the worst kind of bad luck. From behind our lines, the smoke of distant marching columns is spied by the ever watchful Thomas as he stands with Harker's brigade of Wood's division, and he sends a scout to find out who it is. If it is the enemy, we are encircled and dead at best, captive at worst and heading to Andersonville Prison. Clearly it is a huge force of men. The other reinforcements he has called for during the Battle of Chickamauga—Negley's and Sheridan's—never came. Why think that this time is going to be different? But it is our men from the rear, not the ones who fled but Gordon Granger's reserve corps from Rossville led by General Steedman's division. They come because so many others have fled, because it is clear from the sounds of battle that Thomas is still on the field. The scout rides furiously back, dodging bullets, accompanied by another rider carrying the flag of Granger's corps.

Twenty minutes later, the clasp of Steedman's hand seems to impart fresh strength to General Thomas. His eyes lighten with a relieved smile even as his voice keeps the stern control of a general in charge: "General Steedman, I have always been glad to see you, but never so glad as now. How many muskets have you got?" Steedman replies that he has seven thousand five hundred, and General Thomas solemnly says, "It is a good force, and needed very badly."

But Steedman also brings twenty-five more rounds of ammunition for every man still standing, and we all feel that there is now some hope we may survive this bloodbath. His men charge over to the right side of our line where, even at that moment, Brannan's right with my regiment is shaking under waves of Confederate attacks. The shout of the reinforcements matches any Rebel yell, and Steedman himself catches up a regiment's flag and rides forward. "Go back, boys, go back," he yells, "but the flag can't go with you." The men cheer, and join him. His own horse shot from under him, and breaking his arm as he falls, he still leads on foot.

Enemies are fighting with the stones on the ground. Steedman even pelts our men with stones if they waver in the attack.

Over one thousand of his seven thousand five hundred fall in that first exchange after their arrival at Horseshoe Ridge, at the end of Snodgrass Hill.

Thomas could see all this clearly, across a ravine, two

hundred yards away. The attacks never let up in front of him, but he stands immovable as he gazes at Steedman's men. Not a muscle on his face moves. He continues to issue orders in calm, measured tones. It is an extraordinary moment. The love and respect for his men that day—his own, or Wood's, or Negley's, or Granger's, it doesn't matter—his love and respect is clear. He is redeeming the North for all of its horrible mistakes those two days in September, and he is doing it as general after general gives up or refuses to send reinforcements when asked. It is Granger who comes to his aid, unasked, out of a deep regard for Thomas and his determined stand. And all the while Thomas' regular divisions of Baird and Reynolds, with help from Palmer's of Crittenden's corps, continue to hold the line on the left, along Lafayette Road, where the morning's fighting has raged. What respect we felt for Thomas! That day we could feel what he stood for, even if we could only express it in violence.

But Steedman's arrival does not end the battle, much less win it. Our men on the Hill are still outnumbered two to one. Steedman only holds things even, and Longstreet, it turns out, has more in store—an entire division he has not yet used. At three-thirty, there is a lull in the battle and we can see those fresh troops marching through the fractured ranks of Longstreet's earlier divisions and up the southern slope of Snodgrass Hill. Echelons of battalions, handsome and young, possibly heading into their first great battle. This is the last of Longstreet's attacks and the bloodiest.

As they move forward, as if on parade, our artillery opens up with deadly accuracy. Yet Longstreet's men do not fire until they are less than forty paces from our lines. By then our cannon have created huge gaps in their lines, but no one is wavering. At the crest of Snodgrass Hill, they stop, open fire, and for more than an hour, without advance or retreat, gray and blue soldiers fire volley upon volley into each other's ranks.

It is somehow fitting that the regiments that bear the brunt of the last Rebel attack are the very regiments who first arrived on the Hill four hours earlier—the 82nd Indiana, 9th Ohio, and 2nd Minnesota—the best of Brannan's decimated ranks. When the color bearer of the 82nd examined his flag after the battle, it had been pierced by eighty-three Confederate balls. Union soldiers survive by rifling the ammunition boxes of their killed and wounded comrades, after using up the ninety-five thousand rounds that Steedman brought. Confederate colors are planted on the hill, in plain sight of our men. It outrages us that those colors still stand an hour later. As the afternoon wanes, the long shadows made by the declining sun clash with the orange reflections off the swords being waved by desperate commanders.

Finally the dusk settles things for that day. Our men have the advantage of fighting behind breastworks that they improve as the day goes on. They turn away all twenty-five of Longstreet's charges, the last two with only bayonets.

But they cannot win this battle; they are horribly outnumbered and nearly surrounded.

All General Thomas can hope for is to avoid the worst disaster an army can experience. By the end of the day, he knows he has been left on the field to win or lose alone. They won't remember Rosecrans, McCook, Crittenden, Sheridan, Davis, and Negley. They will remember the one who was there for the final loss, who was later called "The Rock of Chickamauga."

General Thomas once told me that battles are won inside oneself, not outside. He said that if you put a plank six inches off the ground, everyone will cross it; if you put the same plank one hundred feet above the ground, hardly anyone will cross it. The moral lies in how you perceive the plank, not in the plank itself, which has not changed in the least. That day, on Snodgrass Hill, the Rebels raised the plank to one hundred feet—or higher—and General Thomas led us across.

❈❈❈

"After your men get the horses settled in the ravine," he told me when he had arrived, "take them over to the right, at the end of the line on the other knoll, and be the scouts I need in case the enemy spreads out and tries to turn our right side. We cannot let them get to the top of the ridge over there."

I dropped down into the ravine and we moved on the double up the far slope, through dense underbrush, toward the crest of the ridge. I led them boldly, as if to show the confidence Thomas had in me as one of his trusted aides.

As we neared the summit, the trees thinned and the soil became rocky and harder to navigate.

Suddenly I stopped, and signaled my men to stop, too. I could hear our own sounds on the other side of the crest. A Rebel detachment was right there, just out of sight. We fixed bayonets and got ready to charge. I was sure Thomas would want me to take the offensive.

The sounds increased and came closer. Finally, I saw the tops of their colors peek above the rock line and I gave the signal to rush forward and shoot when they came into view.

They did, immediately, hundreds and hundreds of them. We fired the first volley at point blank range, but by the time we reloaded, the equal of five of our volleys tore through my ranks and destroyed half of my remaining men. They writhed in pain as the rest of us leaped behind boulders, holding our colors aloft.

The Rebels were exposed to our view and retreated a hundred yards to regroup. But we were so hopelessly outnumbered I had no idea what to do.

For a moment I wished we had tied our horses in the tree line; they were much too far away to help. We had to find a way to fight against odds we could not possibly defeat.

Five minutes went by. I conferred with my aides and company commanders, those who were left standing. We counted our rounds and guessed that we could last a half hour at most if they threw at us all the men I saw during our first volley. We had no artillery. We were going to have to hold the line until some kind of help arrived. I sent my fleetest aide, Captain Wagner, running back down through the thickets and the ravine to tell Thomas of our situation. Maybe he could spare a brigade to at least buy some more time.

Five minutes was all we got; enemy artillery opened up on us. We were a small target and the cannon shells did little harm, but they kept our heads down while their foot soldiers made their way up the hill. Peering out from behind the boulders, we could see line after line of Rebel infantry pushing toward us, shooting if they caught a glimpse of one of our caps. Every minute I ordered a volley but it had no effect on the pace of their approach. They were relentless. I ordered bayonets fixed; the enemy did the same. We were only twenty paces apart. Every one of my men knew that this was their moment of judgment. You could hear loud prayers and exclamations, good byes to wives and children back home, curses toward enemy soldiers uttering the same good-byes and exclamations. We threw stones at them, and they at us. They were us. We were back in the school playgrounds fighting in the dirt over some meaningless insult. We were angry, very angry, but we also knew that there was something unacceptable about this fight, something deeply unfair. They drew closer. I could see their faces: farm boys, eighteen, twenty years old, defending their homeland somewhere in the South. Mine were the outsiders, lost in a strange land. I stood up to order another volley and was struck in the shoulder by a minnie ball from a soldier not fifteen feet in front of me. It hurt like hell. I still stood, and grabbed our colors from a soldier who was already slumping to the ground. I stood as straight as I could, firing my pistol at the nearest man. My boys were disappearing around me, melting back toward the woods, and the Rebels were charging forward with nothing to stop them. I turned my back to them and started to walk as best I could, using the colors for support, expecting another bullet. Out of the woods fifty paces away charged a mass of blue clad soldiers firing past us at the onrushing Rebels.

General Steedman rode at their front and reached down and grabbed the colors out of my grip. I toppled over. Looking up, I heard him curse my men as they retreated: "Go back, boys, go back; but the flag can't go with you." And his own men rushed past me, cheered by his grand courage. I did not lose consciousness. I stumbled down through the tree line and the mass of Steedman's men still coming up the ridge. I tried to look across the ravine to Snodgrass Hill. Too much smoke. Too dizzy. But finally got to a rock that I could lean my back against, protected from the battle above, with a view of Brannan's other troops. I could see him clearly, General Thomas. He was standing still, looking right at me from two hundred yards away, talking to whoever came to him for orders, but never moving his head, never taking his eyes off Horseshoe Ridge.

We rode together during that remarkable withdrawal of our troops to Chattanooga. My wound was treated, the bullet passed right through, and I put my arm in a sling.

That melancholy march back through McFarland's Gap and Rossville was no more than a retreat if it were not for the fact that it should have been a rout. Thomas engineered our withdrawal from the wilds of Georgia with as much care as he trained his men to fight; he had brought off all his wounded. He was not melancholy, at least he did not show it, though he must have wondered how it all fell to him to move an army of exhausted and wounded men without more loss of life. The road was lined for miles with the broken bodies of our soldiers, many near death, calling for company from their regiments in their final minutes. Otherwise, all was quiet, not a sound from thousands of trudging soldiers.

He said nothing to me for miles. He was busy directing his aides with messages for one brigade commander after another.

Once he knew General Baird had left the battlefield and a rear guard was in place, he seemed to relax and become more thoughtful. He spoke first.

"How do you feel, William."

"All right, General."

"Check into the hospital in Chattanooga."

"Yes, General."

"Did you lose many men?"

"Many."

"Do you feel we lost this battle?"

"Yes."

"Yes, I do, too."

On that ride back to Chattanooga, I knew my life was changed forever, and that it was not the war that did it. The war would leave me where it left all my men—dead, or so hurt in spirit that any cause seemed rather hollow. When the war was over—if the Union was saved—we might feel patriotic. We certainly did not that night.

No, what had changed, I felt, was only in me, and in a way I could not explain or bear until later. Whatever he may have felt or said, General Thomas had seen me, across that ravine, at my worst.

But he was kind. And for the first time in my life, I began to feel proud that I had done my best, even if history said that we had failed.

6

We spent two months starving in Chattanooga. My own wound had time to heal, but the food got so bad that half of my horses died in the streets and fields and our men would scour the ground for anything that looked like a kernel of grain to eat. The dead, emaciated horses would be butchered, too, and dried on the hoof. Bragg should have pursued us right after Chickamauga; instead, he chose to let us settle into Chattanooga and hold siege, hoping to starve us to death.

When General Grant was given command of all the Western armies and was on his way to Chattanooga, he cabled George Henry Thomas and told him to hold the city at all costs. Thomas snapped back, "We will hold the town till we starve," to remind Grant of the character of his troops at Chickamauga and of the reality of life in Chattanooga. To retreat from that city, fortified and not yet attacked by the enemy, was inconceivable to Thomas, even if his men were starving.

Chattanooga was a strange place that winter. You could not ask for a more beautiful setting at the bend of the Tennessee

River and the foot of the mountains. It was Indian land only thirty years before, so none of the stately mansions in town had been there very long. The place felt undeveloped, rushed. New wharves, ten-year old train tracks, a large train station that had just been finished—houses rising out of the ground as if they had been dropped in that place from heaven with no concern about their surroundings. And by the time we had starved for a month, those beautiful estates, long abandoned by their Southern sympathizers, looked decrepit as well. Soldiers moved in, and trees and fences came down to provide the wood for countless fires in every marble fireplace. Starving mules ate all the bushes. If the Rebels were going to let us occupy their town, that queenly city of fine residences was not going to be left the way we got it. When relief finally came to our hungry troops, Chattanooga was a bleak and sorrowful place.

Some men deserted, of course, but there was still discipline. General Sheridan caught two of them, and, with the band playing and in front of the assembled troops, he marched them behind their own coffins, carried by their comrades. After they prayed with the chaplain, Sheridan had them sit on the coffins and wait while the detail assigned to shoot got ready. All fired on command, and each of the prisoners fell back over his coffin, dead. General Sheridan on his horse, in full uniform, did not alter his expression.

That night, General Thomas, who witnessed the executions, simply said to me that he preferred drumming deserters out of the army with a brand on their face: "Death is a quick relief, but the shame that comes with that branding is a terrible, inescapable fate."

Into the distressed city came Grant, looking like anything but a commanding general: covered in mud and walking with a crutch after a fall from his horse in New Orleans, military coat unbuttoned to the neck, no sword or belt, his army slouch hat low on his forehead and his head down, a constant cigar clamped between his teeth. There was nothing about him that suggested a commander. Except the feeling that he could not be distracted from what had to be done. And that moral considerations were irrelevant.

The night he arrived it had been raining all day. He had made his way down from Louisville where Secretary of War Stanton had met him and put him in charge. The last sixty miles were on horseback over frontier country west of Chattanooga. He had to circle around the guns on Raccoon Mountain. At the end, the road was knee-deep in mud. Grant even had to be carried at times by his two staff officers when his horse would slip in the quagmire. All along the road lay the bodies of horses and mules. It was October 23, 1863, five days before Thomas' men opened the way to Bridgeport and the starvation ended.

What Grant saw that night was a death camp without injuries, full of crazed and emaciated soldiers under the distant lights of Rebel campfires.

General Thomas met him at his one-story headquarters on Walnut and Fourth streets with what seemed like coldness to Grant's aides. Compared to Grant, Thomas was dapper and polished. And the commander covered in mud from his all-day ride only made the contrast more glaring still. Many months later, Thomas conceded to me that his manners escaped him that night. He did not even notice how bedraggled and wet Grant was. Only after one of the commander's staff pointed it out to Thomas did he jump to his feet and recover his usual graciousness. Regardless, Grant seemed unconcerned, except about Thomas' plans to relieve his men's starvation. Time was short, and only one day's ammunition remained if the Confederates did attack.

Everybody wanted to talk later about the differences between Thomas and Grant, why they were not going to get along. But I was struck by their similarities. In both of them there was a strange combination of personal modesty and iron-like determination. Perhaps Grant cared less about appearances. But neither man wanted to be judged on anything but his performance when the battle came, although each had his own idea of what that performance meant.

❦❦❦

I particularly remember the first dinner they had together, after Grant had spent three nights at Thomas' headquarters while his own headquarters were being readied on First Street. Thomas had me and one of his aides accompany him to Grant's house. What followed was one of those remarkable events of war—a conversation that convinces you that you have looked into the soul of a soldier—both of them.

Grant, much smaller than Thomas, took the offensive over a glass of sherry: "Why did you turn down Stanton's first request a month ago to replace Rosecrans? Did you think he had done a good job, George, at Chickamauga? He had left you in the field. And you refused to replace Buell last year, too. Don't tell me you did not think you were a better commander than either of those incompetents."

"That is my own business, General," Thomas replied. "I did what I felt I had to do: train and protect the men assigned to me. I will never curry favor with politicians against my commander."

"Then how did you imagine you would advance in this army when every promotion means pleasing some politician? The

President is not just a politician, by the way, he is the Commander in Chief of the armies."

"No matter. I will not be accused of self-seeking. I went into this army to train men by my own example. I can do that whether I command the Army of the Cumberland or not."

"That's true. But won't your army spend its time sacrificing itself for the mistakes of the general above you whom you refuse to publicly criticize or replace? What kind of example is that, General?"

"It is the only kind I can control, General Grant. I will protect my men, and give an example to all other generals by doing what I am doing. They proved themselves when they held that hill at Chickamauga, my own men and others."

Grant paused, then struck the harshest chord he could find: "But how is that caring about your men, what you are so famous for?"

Thomas stiffened and stared directly into Grant's eyes.

"I will plan any attack with you, General Grant, and I will never criticize you to your superiors or my inferiors. If your orders fail, I will remain silent. If my orders succeed, I will remain silent. I care only for turning my men into fighters and not sacrificing their lives unnecessarily. You mistake me if you think I am not ambitious. I certainly should be glad to command an army; but I wish it distinctly understood that I am not comfortable, under any circumstances, taking the command held by another general, no matter the errors he's made. We all make errors. I have made my share. You, General Grant, have undoubtedly made yours, and I was not comfortable replacing you at Shiloh."

Grant weighed his words.

"General Thomas, you are a very popular commander. I read the papers, you know. And they influence me, too. One of the reasons I wanted you in charge of the Army of the

Cumberland is your public reputation; people think you walk on water, and if your soldiers only half believe that, then they will serve my purposes in Chattanooga. But how well do you know your own motives? I pride myself on knowing exactly what I want and, most of the time, what it will take to get it. But you want it both ways. Do not misunderstand me, I think you are an excellent fighter; I had no other man in mind to take Rosecrans' place. Are you really telling me that training your men to fight is your true purpose and that you have no interest in recognition from people you disdain?"

"That is what I am saying."

"Then why should I trust a man like that?"

"Why should you not? I will never betray you or my country. I will never let down my men."

"Is that what you think is the basis of trust between one officer and his next in command?"

"Yes, by all means, that is exactly what it should be."

"But who has no interest in glory, especially someone who is getting a lot of it? Look, George, we will work well together; your troops are stalwart, I am sure, as they were at Chickamauga. I am not worried about you letting me down. But you need to learn how to be a realist and a bastard. Idealism has no place in this war. I am uncomfortable with anyone who operates on a principle I cannot comprehend, a false humility that puts his men in danger from superiors you know are incompetent."

Thomas glared: "You have no right to say that, General. There is nothing I care as much about as the fighting ability of my men and their getting home, victorious, to their families and farms. My self-interest and the honor of my men leave no room for anything else. Why should that be a sin in anyone's eyes?"

"I will tell you, General, and we will talk no more about it tonight; my aide has signaled that our dinner is ready. Our job, your job, is to win this war against an enemy that has forfeited his right to exist under a system that is different than the one we are fighting for. Perhaps I understand this better than you; I am from Illinois, not Virginia."

Grant rose and went into dinner, without looking back. Thomas had not moved.

That Grant could make the general I so admired defend his military record, a general so beloved by his men, left me distraught. But it was the clearest demonstration I had seen of the two sides of George Henry Thomas, the proud, principled leader who supported his troops, and the self-effacing, deferential general who had twice refused more power when it was offered him. In his mind, he remained superior to this priggish bully of a man who knew how to use the war for his own aggrandizement.

Thomas and the chief engineer of the Army of the Cumberland, Baldy Smith, had figured out a risky but brilliant solution to our starvation, and Grant had to agree. The west side of town rested on the Tennessee River. Across the river was a one-mile-wide neck of land that could only be crossed by a little country road that wound through hills before it reached the Tennessee River on the other side of the neck. Above this peninsula hovered Lookout Mountain and Raccoon Mountain, both manned by thousands of Bragg's troops ever since we retreated to Chattanooga. Bragg even had troops in the valley between the mountains, near Brown's Ferry, where the road came out on the other side of the hills.

Our side also had General Joseph Hooker and five thousand troops behind Raccoon Mountain in Bridgeport. If he could attack

Brown's Ferry at night from the rear, and Thomas could quietly ferry his men up the Tennessee from the south across the foot of Lookout Mountain, they might storm the Rebels in the valley and take out the artillery on Raccoon Mountain. That would leave only the artillery on Lookout Mountain, and it was too far away—two miles—to be accurate. Then it would only take a heavy pontoon bridge across the Tennessee and all the supplies our troops needed could come in from Bridgeport.

The Army of the Cumberland:
Hazen's Brigade Landing Below Lookout Mountain

At midnight on October 27th, a thousand men, myself included, climbed into fifty pontoons eight miles above the bend in the river before you got to Brown's Ferry. In a slight fog, we moved out without making a sound, except for the muffled slap of the oars. Cavalrymen, like me, were laughing quietly about serving as infantry, and not even on the land! Silence was the order of the day, as our boat commanders constantly reminded us in whispers. We stayed close to the western shoreline, without lanterns, and tried to cope as quietly as we could with the sharp branches that occasionally swept our faces.

As we slowly swung around the tip of Moccasin Point, we expected, surely, to be seen by Rebel sentries on the other side of the Tennessee River. But no sound or gun shots came out of the dark, despite a full moon and the lifting mist. Only when we reached the ferry itself, and found our own troops on the peninsula waiting with even more pontoons, did we begin to realize that our starvation might soon be over.

But that was the very moment we were certain to be seen, and the Rebel pickets at the foot of Raccoon Mountain opened up. We frantically maneuvered the pontoons, all at the same time in the most wonderful chaos, across the Tennessee River and into position, as our artillery, that Thomas had already put on the peninsula, rained cannon balls over our heads to the far bank. In the dark it was amazing how quickly we could paddle and then link those pontoons together, building outward to the center from both sides of the river. In one hour, with minnie balls regularly peppering the water around us, a pontoon bridge had been created from Brown's Ferry to the peninsula. By morning, the food wagons from Bridgeport, Alabama could move across that bridge and up the country road over Moccasin Point, and reach our poor emaciated soldiers. After October 28th, no Union soldier in Chattanooga was going to starve. Our jubilation overcame us, and what began as muffled cheering became shouts and hollers, and a general whooping and backslapping. We had done it! And we had only lost twenty-nine men to death and injury.

The plan had worked perfectly, and General Thomas was seen laughing out loud and doing a jig in front of his officers—and Grant himself—when the news came through. His men were going to survive, Thomas yelled, and to hell with Bragg!

Nevertheless, a few days later Grant found a chance to embarrass Thomas when he ordered him, without the possibility of horse-drawn artillery support, to attack the Rebels' right at the northern end of Missionary Ridge to the east of the city. Grant had been pestered by telegrams from the Secretary of War worrying over the North's ability to hold Knoxville after Bragg sent troops in that direction. He thought that an action against Bragg's flank would draw those Confederate troops back to Chattanooga. But Thomas could not attack Bragg without uncovering Chattanooga itself. Thomas protested vehemently that it would be a willful sacrifice of his men, and Grant countermanded his order. But it gave Grant the opportunity he needed to criticize Thomas and the Army of the Cumberland for being immovable and too protective of each other.

We were immovable, though not in the way Grant meant it: we were in those same positions so long that our men and the Rebels across the river got to know each other well. Even Grant, when he took his first tour of the lines, was greeted by a salute on the Rebel shoreline instead of sniper shots.

❦❦❦

Once the starvation ended after the first month or so, we got to enjoy camp life; it seemed like nothing was going to change—no attack from the Rebs, and no way for us to get up and over the mountains. Might as well begin to have some fun, we thought.

So Chaplain Strong and some of the boys started having regular cotillion parties in camp. On the parade ground, Negro servants played their fiddles and gentlemen went through honors-to-partners and circle-all with as much pleasure as if their partners had on pink dresses and white slippers.

But after a cotillion, the chaplain always sang the same hymn, our taps for the night and a reminder of the war:

> Perhaps He will admit my plea,
> Perhaps will hear my prayer;
> If I must perish I will pray
> And only perish here.
>
> I will not perish if I go
> To His true Heaven on high;
> But if I choose to stay, I know,
> I must forever die.

These old hymns sound in our ears, and we are almost tempted to give ourselves to death. Nothing can make us forget earth and its troubles as these old church songs, a sacred refrain on which, some day, our souls will float away to a better country.

The Crutchfield House was the only decent hotel in Chattanooga, at least the only one Union officers seemed to treat with respect. It was here that they accommodated their guests if they did not want to lodge them at headquarters. Five days after Grant's countermanded order for Thomas to attack the Confederate right on Missionary Ridge, General Thomas asked me to accompany him to Crutchfield House on an important matter.

Waiting for us in the plush dining room was a regal woman in a lavender satin dress. She immediately rose as we entered and moved toward us.

"Colonel Swain," Thomas said confidently, "I would like to introduce my wife, Frances Kellogg Thomas. She has made the long trip from New York at my request."

"I am so glad to make your acquaintance, Colonel Swain. General Thomas has told me how much he has trusted in your confidence since Stone River. I want to thank you for being a such a support to my husband."

As we adjourned to the dining room, it was already clear that they were well suited. Tall and stately, they moved together, instinctively, with a grace that seemed to fill the air.

"How did you meet?" I asked Mrs. Thomas as we were settling into our chairs. Her expressive dark eyes turned to the general.

"I so enjoy telling this story, do you mind, dear?

"Not at all, Frances," the general replied. "In fact, I may add some memories of my own. Revisiting happier times will be a welcome diversion for two weary soldiers."

It was obvious that Frances Thomas was an educated, highly intelligent woman. There was such self-possession in her voice as she began to speak:

"My widowed mother, younger sister Julia, and I were residing at the West Point Hotel for the Spring and Summer season in eighteen fifty-two. The weather was glorious that year and we spent our days boating on the Hudson, walking or hiking much of the two hundred acres at West Point, and also partaking in the social life at the Academy. My cousin Lyman Kellogg was a cadet there and kept us informed of the minstrel shows, concerts, and especially the hops, which were the dances where eligible young ladies could meet eligible cadets. My mother was becoming a bit distressed regarding my matrimonial prospects, but I was determined to marry for more than just financial security. My father had been a successful hardware merchant in Troy, New York, so I could be more selective, if somewhat stubborn, in my attitude.

"Soon after our arrival in April, we received an invitation from Lyman to attend a Saturday night hop. It was an electrifying evening—graduation was close at hand, the cadets were splendid in uniform, and the mess hall had been transformed for the occasion with laurel branches shading the windows and the support pillars encircled with muskets and bayonets. They even had candled sconces first used at a ball during the Revolutionary War. The transformation was remarkable."

"It was as though time stood still when she entered the room," Thomas quickly added. "I had been appointed Instructor of Artillery and Cavalry at the Academy in fifty-one, and most Saturday nights I would be preparing for the classes I taught. Even though dance instruction was part of the curriculum, I made little use of it. But Cadet Kellogg requested my presence that evening and I acquiesced. He was one of my favorite students.

"I saw Frances across the room even before her cousin introduced us. She was resplendent in her deep coral gown. I remember it because it was such an unusual color. The dancing was so lively that night—beside waltzing, we danced quadrilles, polkas, gallops, and lanciers, and I was finally grateful that I had paid attention in all those Academy dance classes. At the end of the evening I was so sure of my feelings and my future. All I had to do now was court her and convince her that marrying me was a good idea."

There was such tenderness in his voice as he spoke. His love and admiration were unmistakable.

"And courted me he did," she said, smiling. "The rest of my stay at West Point was filled with as much time with George as he could manage. My favorite moments were spent on Flirtation Walk, a romantic promenade that winds along the Hudson. That is where I received George's spooney button from inside his uniform jacket. I knew what it meant since every young lady anticipates being given one as a sign of a cadet's intention, and George still had his from his days as a student. Please try to understand, Colonel Swain, what it means to a thirty-one-year old woman to be betrothed to a man she actually loves and admires. I thought my heart would burst. I would not be a spinster and I did not compromise my values!

"We were married in Troy ten years ago this November. George wore the sword presented to him by his Southampton County, Virginia neighbors for his service in Mexico and Florida. With its ornate silver, scrollwork, and gemstones, it was more beautiful than my gown! After a wedding tour to New York City, George was assigned to Fort Yuma in Arizona, the first of many separations between us. But I am so proud, Colonel Swain, to be his wife. I will endure whatever is necessary for my husband to do what is required for our nation."

I was struck by her strength and resolve. I knew they had little time together and that the general did not bring her to camp as the other officers continually brought their wives. This was their first meeting in two years.

We ordered the best food and wine available that night, in honor of her arrival. Conversation flowed freely. Seeing the general so animated and relaxed was a much needed respite from the stark reality of our lives. Chattanooga was a devastated town, but that meal was the finest I had in the entire war.

When dinner was over, I bid them good night and walked away wondering if I would ever be held in such esteem by Neala. To me, that had become as important as love.

Two days later, Mrs. Thomas was spirited out of Chattanooga under nightfall, just as she had been spirited in. I could tell the other generals were amazed. They brought in their wives when camp life was boring and no battles were on the horizon. After years apart General Thomas had brought his wife into a dangerous spot when a battle was imminent.

When she was gone, a gloom settled for a while on Thomas and the rest of us. It was as if, when she left, some of his hopes did, too. And Grant did not help matters in planning the battle for Missionary Ridge by giving the Army of the Cumberland only a supporting role. Thomas seemed resigned to losing his chance at a victory in Chattanooga that would make up for the loss the army endured at Chickamauga. We wanted desperately to vindicate ourselves, but we could feel our spirits drop.

Through all that gloom, Neala was so dutiful about her letter writing. It was obvious that she was a woman of her word, and she kept me apprised of all the news in Vernon. I wrote, when I could, letters full of admiration for my soldiers and especially General Thomas. I was prudent about my ardor for her, and kept my feelings about her to myself, hoping that time and fate would be on my side.

Again the general called me to his tent for more than the

next day's battle plan. This time it was the sound of rain outside, not the usual singing of the troops.

"It is hard to deal with their lack of trust, William. We deserve more after Chickamauga."

"I agree, sir. You showed your loyalty there. It's clear that Grant won't trust a general from Virginia. How can you tolerate being so distrusted, especially after your own family disowned you for serving your country?"

"William, I know exactly what the requirements are for the victory that will end this war and save lives, the lives of boys from Southampton County as well as boys from the North, if they would just let me do the job I can do—crush the Southern army. You cannot repeat this. So many of the generals on both sides, when they are not completely incompetent, are without any notion of how to win. They watch boy after boy go to his death with no justification except, 'There is the enemy, shoot him!'"

"But, sir, if you truly believe that you know what to do, why did you turn down promotions that would have allowed you to do it?"

"Don't think I haven't revisited those decisions, William, especially since my harrowing dinner with Grant. He is a typical Northerner: boorish and rude, present company excepted, of course. It is an evening like that that makes me proud of being a Southern gentleman. West Point favored us with their rules of etiquette; my friends and I were in our glory there—teaching those Northern boys how to be proper men. But now, I'm on the other side, representative of a dying way of life, a gentility and connection to the land that my colleagues can never understand. I will not stop being who I was raised to be, but mostly I feel like the rooster in the hen house that has been invaded by coyotes. I'm the top dog but not in their pack!

"I won't turn down another promotion, William. Grant was

right about one thing: I have to relinquish my civility toward failed generals and get on with the business of war.

"But I have to be honest with myself, too. I miss the Southern earth that soothed my soul. I miss being recognized by my friends. I miss Robert E. Lee."

7

We were interrupted by the murmur of men watching an eclipse of the moon that made the campfires of the two enemies even brighter and more eerie. I bid the general good night and joined the soldiers who looked on in awe and wondered what the omen meant. We tried to persuade ourselves that it was bad for the Rebels, not us. Up on the mountains they were closer to the disappearing moon, closer to the darkness that had descended on all of us.

Either way, we knew it meant there was no turning back; the battle at Missionary Ridge we had been awaiting for two months was here.

Sherman on the left of our line was to attack the right flank of the Confederates on November 21st along the ridge, similar to what Thomas had refused to do earlier in the month. This time Chattanooga would be protected by Thomas himself as a decoy, while Sherman and Hooker pinched the Rebel forces from the two ends.

The trouble was that Sherman did not even get to the battle until the 23rd, because Grant's intelligence operatives had missed all the ravines and valleys that Sherman's columns would have to traverse. So, lo and behold, it was Thomas after all who started the first day's attack the afternoon of the 23rd of November by moving toward Missionary Ridge and capturing Orchard Knob, a mile in front of the Rebel lines. It was still a diversion to draw Bragg's attention away from his flanks, but it was not supposed to be the army's first move. We met very little resistance when we emerged from the woods at the foot of the hill, and even captured a number of Alabama troops who seemed surprised by our finally beginning to do something. Grant told us to hold fast, and get ready for the real battle the next day.

But Sherman was still not ready then or even by the end of the 24th. Bragg had noticed the massing of troops on his right and moved Hardee and Cleburne, his best fighters, to stop Sherman. They did. But Bragg also ignored his left flank on Lookout Mountain, and on the same day Sherman was being stalled to the north, Hooker's ten thousand men were charging at will up Lookout Mountain against only seven thousand Rebels. The way was so steep that Rebel cannons could not be tipped sharply enough to hit Hooker's men. Down in the valley on Orchard Knob, we watched and, when the battle went above the cloud line, tried to hear how it was progressing. The flash of guns was like lighting in the sky.

Grant's plan of action had been turned on its head. Sherman, his favorite, was being humiliated, Thomas, his decoy, had moved forward prematurely and easily, and Hooker, his secondary attack, was succeeding beyond expectations. And when dawn came on the 25th, we could see the union flag on the prow of Lookout Mountain. We needed badly to share in Hooker's success, even though there were fifteen thousand enemy troops in front of us, not the seven thousand that Hooker had defeated.

But Grant refused to change his plan. He still wanted Sherman to have the glory, so he took another five thousand of our men away to support him. Now it was completely clear to Thomas and his men that we were not to play an important role in the battle for Missionary Ridge. It was clear to Bragg, too, who had shifted two more divisions against Sherman away from Lookout Mountain, even before Hooker got to the top.

Grant stood with Thomas on Orchard Knob as word came back on the 25th that Sherman was completely stalled in one ravine after another. Finally, grudgingly, Grant suggested that the Army of the Cumberland should attack the center of the Rebel forces, dug in from the bottom to the top of Missionary Ridge. It was three in the afternoon and Sherman was still asking for more help; at least Thomas' men might take the rifle pits at the base of the ridge and convince the Rebels that the all-out attack was now going to come from the center, even if it was not. I can remember Grant saying, one more time, "We must do something for Sherman."

Our men, mine fighting now on foot, had been arming themselves for two days, waiting for an opportunity, no matter how foolhardy, to redeem themselves after Chickamauga. Every orderly, cook, and clerk had found himself a gun. We heard the artillery open up at three-forty, only two hours before dark. We were as ready as any soldiers ever were to fight. I quickly rode down to join them in front of Missionary Ridge.

But instead of sending us forward when Grant finally gave him the order, George Henry Thomas did the most remarkable thing. He put us in parade formation, and marched us back and forth, behind our battle flags, as if we were on review. He used exactly the same drills he made us practice five times a week for the past year, we knew each step by heart. And it gave us the confidence we needed, as if General Thomas was reminding us of what we had learned under him, telling us that he was sure of our desire but needed us to remember what to do with that desire. It worked. The sniper fire from the ridge in front of us ceased for twenty minutes as we marched in review. I believe they were impressed, too, or at least stunned into silence.

I stayed on horseback when my cavalry joined the infantry. From my higher vantage, the sight of eighteen thousand men moving with perfect regularity as they mounted an impossible vertical attack filled me with awe. I had never in my life seen such obedience and faith in any commander. We would do whatever he asked, exactly as he asked.

After twenty minutes the bugle sounded, the sniper fire suddenly began again, and Thomas swung his forces into lines of attack. It would have been easier if the Rebel troops were all the way up the five-hundred-foot ridge looming over us. But they were at the bottom, in the middle, and on the top: every break in the ascent was ringed with entrenchments. And there were almost no trees on the rise for us to take cover behind. Even before the battle, Missionary Ridge was barren, and what trees had been there were felled for Rebel breastworks. Picture that stark ridge running for several miles and our lines, with leveled bayonets, advancing in double ranks as long as the ridge itself. Never before in the war had the two enemies confronted each other across a front so open and so wide. Pickett's charge at Gettysburg was narrow by comparison.

But remember, we were only supposed to take the rifle pits at the base. We did that, with one thousand prisoners to boot, eagerly killing those Rebs who did not surrender or fled up the slope toward the next line of entrenchments. The side of the mountain was aflame with artillery explosions from both sides. The Confederate artillery started to enfilade our ranks with canister as soon as we stopped at the rifle-pits: we either had to go back or go forward. So, even with our knapsacks and winter coats, we clawed our way up, foot by foot, to rock after rock. We were wild—I have never seen soldiers so unaffected by the death falling around them. I left my mount at the rifle pits and a few feet further on I remember stopping and looking to the right and left at my men, still in order, gradually ascending the slope, completely unaware or uncaring if one of their comrades next to them fell or cried out. They were not unaware or uncaring, and when we reached the top they asked about every one of the men who fell—they had seen it all. But nothing was going to distract them from what they were doing on the way up. We were in a trance. Pushing, pushing up the next rise, catching a breath when we could, ignoring the wounds we suffered. On that entire ascent I was never hit, but every man around me fell and got up again, some more than once. My hands were bloody from the sharp rocks, and many of us were covered with others' blood when we finally reached the Ridge. We hit the top in six different places at the same time.

The most startling sight going up was to see all ranks rising together—privates, generals, colonels, all ranks side by side in no particular order. I could not believe how injured some men were. How could someone with an arm dangling and just waiting to be amputated get to the top as fast as someone who was whole and unwounded? Or a color bearer be the first up when the elevation was the steepest we ever saw and it was far easier for a soldier with a rifle to go up than someone carrying a fifty-pound flag? Sheridan was the first general to the top, I was told, emptying his flask in one gulp and throwing it at the fleeing Rebels. We even turned their cannon on them as they rushed down the other side of the ridge. That was the final surprise—that the Rebels no longer fought when we got to the top. I suppose they figured that anyone who could get up that slope in a hail of gunfire could not be defeated if the ground was level. It surely was not that the Rebels did not have troops there: we lost more men coming up than they had lost shooting down on us. At least three thousand of them were captured on the ridge, and behind those who did run was a trail of muskets, blankets, and knapsacks. Night fell. Pursuing them became too difficult. We were too happy, too relieved that we had made up for Chickamauga. This time, a full moon seemed to bless our celebration. It took us one hour to take that Ridge, one hour! From the parading of our troops, to the taking of the rifle-pits, to the struggle up the five hundred feet to the summit, just sixty minutes!

The Army of the Cumberland:
General Baird's Division Capturing Rebel Guns

When General Thomas got there a half hour later, we surrounded his horse, all talking at once. His face colored through his graying beard and he nodded when one of his men simply said, "This is what you trained us for, General." Sherman's troubles let up only with the general Confederate retreat. But here was Thomas, paid back for Chickamauga, his men opening a way out of his thankless reputation as a defender of an army he had never been allowed to lead.

Grant had finally put him in charge, but General Granger told me he heard Grant mutter, back on Orchard Knob, when Thomas' men reached the summit: "Damn the battle, I had nothing to do with it."

⋖⋗⋖⋗⋖⋗

Hours later I joined Thomas in his tent down in the valley. The whole town and its surrounding hills were ours; excited cables were being fired off to the War Department and the eastern newspapers. No one could believe that so much could be accomplished with so little loss of life; everyone thought that this, with Gettysburg, were the turning points of the war.

I knew he had not ordered the charge all the way to the top, no one had. I knew that Sheridan was going to get more glory than anyone else.

But it was clear that Thomas had loved the fact that Grant's plan for taking Missionary Ridge, which did not include him, was turned upside down by his own men. Up on the crest of the Ridge, Thomas was proud of us; he had rushed to share our enjoyment.

"My men did well, very well. I expected many to die, and they did not. It is what I prayed for."

He paused and took a breath.

"...even though it cannot make up for Chickamauga."

A week later, on his own authority, he designated Orchard Knob a national military cemetery, and directed his men to bury their Northern comrades together, mixing up their states. "Damn states' rights," he said. "I've had enough of it."

That same day I put in for a three weeks' furlough and he signed it, an unusual gesture from a man who hated furloughs and had never taken one himself.

8

I rode over to Bridgeport, and took the train to Nashville. It seemed to take forever; the train went slower than usual since Forrest's cavalry were still marauding somewhere behind Northern lines and the soldiers on board were cautious and watchful. At Nashville, another train took me to the Ohio River where I ferried across to Cincinnati and found a day coach to Vernon. The whole trip lasted four days; it gave me time to prepare for what I had to do.

General Thomas had shown his deeper feelings to me, his love of his wife, his pride in his men, and his Southern roots, but also his resignation. His influence on me was quiet and heartfelt.

When the coach reached the outskirts of Vernon, I got out to walk the rest of the way, slowly, very slowly, kicking up dust with my shuffling feet. It was cold, of course, no snow on the ground, but cold. I squeezed the collar around my neck. My uniform was in the knapsack on my back. You could not be sure I was a soldier.

I felt hopeful and nervous at the same time. I knew people would see me; but they would be seeing me for the first time, I felt. I would have to introduce myself all over again.

I stepped into the *Banner* office to see Jason, my assistant, who had run the paper in my absence. He assured me that all was well; he was only having trouble with the obituaries of his friends who were dying regularly.

"You look different, sir," he said, as he placed my knapsack on the stairs to my apartment above the newspaper. "You shaved your beard. It makes you look younger. I bet Miss Neala will like it."

Just her name gave me more strength for the unannounced visit to my father a few blocks away.

I cleaned myself up and left.

I understood what had to happen before I could do anything else in Vernon, or in my life. I found him behind the same desk in the same office that he had occupied for as long as I could remember, a whiskey bottle in plain sight. He looked up and did not flinch. "What do you want?" he asked.

We had not seen each other for a year, but it seemed an eternity since I had met him face to face. My apprehension disappeared, and I came to the point so quickly that it surprised me. "I have killed men, Father; been shot; been at Chickamauga and Missionary Ridge; done well and done badly, both. I want you to know who I am."

"You are who you are. Live with it. That is what I do," and he poured himself a drink. He did not offer me one.

"I thought I could never forgive you for what you did to my mother and to me, your only son. But I have come to realize that you could not forgive yourself for whatever mistakes you have made in your life. Respecting yourself comes from admitting errors and bearing yourself no malice. Someone has taught me how to do that and I am truly sorry that no one did that for you."

He looked up. "I have no regrets."

There was a long silence. He resumed his work.

I left without saying goodbye.

I was at Nashville when he died the next year, slumped over the same desk.

❖❖❖

I went straight to Neala's father's farm, with its rolling pastures surrounded by one white fence after another, seemingly undisturbed by the war tearing the country apart. Neala was standing on the front porch, as if she knew the moment I would arrive. The look on her face was the most mysterious mixture of joy and apprehension.

She was a sight for sore eyes—dressed as usual in her leather breeches and brother John's riding boots. I loved her independence, though at this moment I desperately wanted her to be as glad to see me as I she.

She greeted me with a handshake. "How are you, William? It has been a long time, and I must be honest and tell you that I missed you terribly and prayed daily for your safety."

For a brief moment I felt that I would lose my composure. With the afternoon sun glistening in her hair, she was more beautiful than I remembered. During our many past conversations, I would always find myself deferring to her, a habit I disliked in myself but could not seem to control. What was odd this time was my own sense of height. It felt like the general's uncommon stature had rubbed off on me.

"Neala, before your presence overwhelms me, I must discuss something of great importance with you. This has been a momentous year in my life. Even though I suffered defeat, was wounded, and lost my trusted horse, I experienced a great victory at Missionary Ridge. Throughout this war, I witnessed such fortitude and loyalty that it has changed me forever. The general who leads us has shown me the true measure of a man and I am ready to take the next step. I love you. I cannot imagine my life without you beside me. In the past I was hesitant to speak of these things but I am finally able. I need to know if you have thought of me in a similar way."

Her dark eyes suddenly looked sorrowful. She motioned for me to sit next to her on the porch steps.

"Of course I have, William. But I cannot proceed or even show you my heart, beyond what you saw in my letters, until I reveal to you some of my own history. Then, if you are still inclined to consider me, we will speak with my father."

And she began.

"As you know, my parents were born in Ireland. My father's family had been horse farmers for several generations and my mother's family were merchants. Both came from Cork in a town called Youghal, where one of my mother's ancestors was the Lord Mayor. Highly unusual since he was Jewish. They had come to Ireland when they were expelled from Spain in the 15th century; their numbers were so few that the Irish treated them well, and so they remained as they do to this day. The one thing that was intolerable was intermarriage between a Jew and a Catholic— bad enough if my father had married a Protestant but a Jew was unthinkable.

"To escape the criticism from both sides they emigrated to America, were married by the ship's captain and settled in Kentucky to raise horses.

"We had a wonderful life there. They joined a Congregational Church that believed in a just and loving god who cared for all of humanity, not just Christians. The church even tolerated criticisms of slavery, and within my own family we would have heated debates about whether Negroes were fully human and our equals. John believed otherwise and died for that belief, remaining true to himself to the end. Thank God, my mother Rachel did not have to endure his loss; she had died of fever two years earlier.

"She was very proud of her religious heritage and we continue to celebrate both the Jewish and Christian holidays. But she was very sensible and believed that protecting her marriage and children surpassed all else. My parents' devotion to one another and their children showed us the true meaning of God's love. I expect to continue her tradition with my own family, and if it has to be of a clandestine nature, as it is now, then so be it. I am my mother's daughter and her legacy will live on with me.

"There you have it, William. Can you accept me as I am? A cross between two distinct cultures, and one of them that evokes fear and distrust in otherwise good people? Sometimes I feel more affiliation with our Negroes, except that my heritage is a secret."

Her vulnerability only served to increase my admiration for her. I gathered her in my arms and reassured her that my love was true and constant; that I could never be persuaded otherwise.

Walking to the paddock where her father was training his horses was exhilarating. With Neala's hand in mine I was able finally to envision a future filled with the assurance of contentment.

Liam expressed his pleasure at our impending union by giving me a hearty slap on the back and a new horse.

"You need a good steed, young man. I've been raising these Saddlebreds for years, and they're fast and smooth as silk to ride. Sixteen and a half hands he is and he'll lie down on command and stay down to protect you. We want you to come home in one piece, son."

The last day of my leave, Neala and I went fishing at the bend of the river at the foot of the road to Du Pont. I did not catch a thing, but I saw all the fish that I missed, and that, somehow, was better.

I left the next day, two days before Christmas, riding on Liam Monaghan's gift to me, and arrived back in Chattanooga on the New Year, 1864.

the army was in the same place I left it weeks before, on the plains between Chattanooga and Missionary Ridge. I had gotten a privilege from him

9

The army was in the same place I left it weeks before, on the plains between Chattanooga and Missionary Ridge. I had gotten a privilege from him in going home that he rarely gave to any of his men, and never took advantage of himself. So I did not know what to expect from my own troops.

Luckily they were still patting themselves on the back for Missionary Ridge, and were not as bored with camp life as they would have been after a loss like Chickamauga. When I arrived in the twilight, the camp was as quiet as could be. Fires were starting up, and I was greeted as if I had not been away. Their thoughts were where I had just come from; maybe my walking among them triggered even more memories of home. And I brought the newspapers from Indianapolis and Chicago that celebrated their charge up Missionary Ridge and how Bragg's "terrible arc of iron was bent back upon itself and crushed like a buzzard's egg." Following Chickamauga, they needed to hear that the rest of the world, like them, had forgotten that defeat.

They told me about their news, too. Thomas was the life of the generals' party at the Crutchfield on New Year's Eve, the night before, after sipping wine for an hour and becoming the center of attention: the affable and gregarious gentleman I had rarely seen. His manners were impeccable. Finally, at long last, Missionary Ridge had loosened him up. The dour general I left after the battle had reached some kind of understanding: "Without my appointment to West Point," he told me, "my life would have been commonplace. I never would have met my wife or understood my talent for war. I have come to accept whatever God grants me."

Even without talking to him I knew that the role for my cavalry regiment was going to be bigger if we pushed toward Atlanta, as we were almost sure to do. The larger the army, the slower it was going to move, and the more important the cavalry action that was certain to transpire. Forrest would pull back to Georgia with Morgan, and our small cavalry forces, mine included, would have their hands full. We would have to prevent the minor assaults of mounted troops that would do more to slow down the Army of the Cumberland than anything the terrain would present. Georgia was rugged enough without having the Rebel cavalry sniping at us every day.

But the start of those arrangements would wait until tomorrow. As night fell, one of my own brigades came into camp after a routine patrol, singing in unison, at the top of their voices:

An exile away from home, splendor dazzles in vain,
Oh, give me my lowly thatched cottage again;
The birds singing gaily, that came at my call,
Give me them, with the peace of mind dearer than all.

Home, home, sweet home,
There is no place like home;
There is no place like home.

⋖⋗⋗⋗⋖⋗

It was March before anything changed in camp. Grant suddenly went to Washington as chief of all the armies, east and west. He immediately appointed Sherman to take over his command of the western armies, including the Army of the Cumberland under Thomas, the Army of the Tennessee under young McPherson, and the Army of the Ohio under Schofield, who would be Thomas' enemy after Nashville. Grant, of course, should have chosen Thomas to replace him in Chattanooga; but by then none of us in Thomas' ranks were surprised when he got passed over one more time. I talked to him that very night, and he seemed strangely composed.

He still valued Sherman as a friend, but he was senior to Sherman and had a far more successful campaign in the West. Sherman had failed early in the war in Kentucky, been surprised at Shiloh, and disappointed Grant's hopes at Chattanooga, whichever way Grant wanted to see it. His great achievement was his hard-driving support for Grant at Vicksburg. Sherman got the western command on his attitude, his similarity to Grant, not on his achievements.

But Thomas did not seem to mind when I found him in his tent after dinner the day Grant and Sherman were promoted.

"I am all right with Sherman, William. And I have realized a great deal. That my men were the best fighters around. The American public knows what they have done, and what I have done to get them ready. There have been plenty of articles in the Nashville and Chattanooga papers about what happened, and giving the Army of the Cumberland the credit.

"My men have begun to realize what they are fighting for. The deeper we get into the South, the larger the plantations and the more Negroes there are still working the fields. No masters or overseers are in sight, but the slaves are so frightened that they do not dare stop. For a few minutes, they will drop their plows and come to the fences for a look at their would-be liberators."

And Thomas had decided, against Sherman's wishes, to use southern Negroes as volunteer soldiers. Grant, too, was against this decision, but Thomas felt that they should be used in war like any individuals of a civilized nation.

Sherman's army finally crept out of Chattanooga in May and inched its way south in the heat and rain toward Atlanta. Ringgold, Dalton, Resaca, New Hope Church—battles, not large, that sent one hundred thousand men slowly moving, skirmishing and digging in, losing more casualties to disease than to bullets. Only when we reached the foot of Kennesaw Mountain outside Marietta, ten miles from Atlanta, did Joe Johnston's forces really turn and Sherman show how little regard he had for Thomas.

But before that—at Dalton—I was shot again. Chasing after Forrest with two hundred men, we got caught at Snake Creek Gap when McPherson decided to pull back without attacking Resaca. Forrest saw our hesitation and came around behind, betting that we would retreat unnecessarily. As I turned my men to lead the way, a volley ripped through my other shoulder and I barely held onto my horse's neck. Two of my lieutenants came up beside and shielded me, and we bolted through the gap with McPherson's artillery pounding the Rebel flanks just in time. Forrest never stayed around for his punishment anyway.

The Battle of Ringgold

Five miles to camp and I had lost a lot of blood. I was in and out of consciousness. I do not know how long it took General Thomas to come to the field hospital; it seemed as if it was right away. His huge figure blocked the light and I could only hear his deep voice: "That is it for you, Colonel Swain. You come back and you are a worse soldier than before you left. What am I going to do with you?" His humor relieved my agony. Then there was a pause, and I heard him add, so quietly, "I can not afford to lose you, William." Years later, J.P. Willard, the general's aide, told me that Thomas left my bed and spent two more hours talking to the other wounded under his command, a habit I knew he employed for the entire war. It meant a great deal to his men and endeared him to us for life.

That wound took me out of commission for Kennesaw Mountain. Thank goodness it did. Because I was spared what Sherman did to Thomas there, which ought to have convinced the general that his friends were worse than his enemies.

⊰⊱⊰⊱⊰⊱

Johnston dug in on Kennesaw Mountain, much as Bragg had done on Missionary Ridge and Lookout Mountain eight months before, but with far more seriousness. Deep trenches, high parapets covering them, fire lanes in front of breastworks, chevaux-de-frise stuck in the ground and pointed in our direction. Sherman positioned Thomas' men in the front as Grant had done in Chattanooga. The difference was that Kennesaw was a lot steeper than Missionary Ridge and thicker with brambles and bushes. And this time Thomas himself went to Sherman with the same kind of plan that Grant had tried to no avail on Missionary Ridge: to swing another force around the wing of the Rebel army, capture Marietta, and attack the enemy from the side, using Thomas' men as a decoy. We had the Confederates on the run, only a few miles from Atlanta; Thomas figured that to rout them now—which was not likely to happen twice from the front, up a steep incline—would leave Atlanta exposed and their army crushed. My men had even been a part of a huge force of cavalry Sherman had pulled together that finally defeated Forrest to the north, where he was threatening our communications to Tennessee.

But Sherman would not listen. He was determined to

send Thomas' men up the mountain, and in one hundred and ten degree heat. He told the Secretary of War, "it may cost us dear." And he was right, so right.

Maybe it was jealousy of his mentor, General Grant, that drove Sherman to try something so foolhardy and dramatic. He is supposed to have cabled Grant just before the assault maligning the Army of the Cumberland as too slow and defensive. Did he send them forward to show Grant what a crack general could get Thomas' men to do, or maybe he was jealous of George Thomas himself, whose military record was far more successful than Sherman's, even though Sherman was Grant's favorite?

Whatever Sherman's reason, Thomas did what he was told, sending his men up the mountain, to their sure destruction. Dan McCook's and Harker's brigades led the way against fifty Confederate cannon, through the smoke of thousands of muskets firing at once. Two hours later, two thousand five hundred of Thomas' men lay killed and wounded. McCook and Harker were dying. "Too bad, too bad," General Thomas angrily muttered looking through his field glasses. His men had gained a little ground, and Sherman pressed him for more. Thomas told him that his soldiers, some of whom got within thirty yards of the Rebel trenches until blocked by the bodies of their comrades, would hold their position as long as they did not have to attack again that day. "One or two more assaults will use up my army."

That night, on June 27th, Sherman changed his mind again, withdrew and began the flanking movement that Thomas had supported from the beginning. When confronted by some of his generals, he simply said, "You have to give up life and blood occasionally to remember what war is about. Losses like this are a small affair, a kind of morning dash."

The soldiers themselves just buried their dead. A line of skirmishers from each side met half way. The enemy then carried our dead on their side to the line, where they were taken by our men and buried. The Rebel dead were treated the same way, taken to the line and passed to the enemy for burial. Some conversations of a cordial nature even took place between officers and men of the opposing parties. The Rebels who deserted received hats and blouses, and were sent home. Even those who resisted and were captured seemed willing to go to Fort Delaware in northern Pennsylvania, our Andersonville, where the daily meat was usually the rats they could kill. But Thomas decided to hold those prisoners until Atlanta fell, and then send them home, too, without weapons, to their families.

Nothing really could stop our army except ourselves. We swept around Kennesaw, taking Marietta without a struggle, cracking Johnston's defenses on the Chattahoochee with little resistance. Hood replaced Johnston and attacked at Peachtree Creek. We lost General McPherson, but once again Thomas' men held against Hardee's fury. General Thomas, wildly stroking the whiskers on his chin, yelled, "Hurrah, look at the Third Division! They're driving them!" Thomas himself had galloped alongside the batteries he had moved up to protect a gap that Sherman had opened in Thomas' lines by shifting men where they were not needed. He ordered the cannons to fire scraps of metal and the Confederate forces wilted. Hardee lost eight thousand men killed and wounded, and the Army of the Cumberland moved within a mile of Atlanta.

Gradually, relentlessly, Sherman closed our massive army around Atlanta, encircling it and cutting off the Rebel lines of communication. On September 1st, two months after Kennesaw Mountain, and four months after the start of the campaign, the Rebels quietly evacuated the city, burning their stores to the ground. Sherman said that Thomas "almost danced in his elephantine way."

Thomas learned a few days later that Sherman would head safely toward Savannah and the sea, and send him on a more thankless and dangerous voyage. I made it back from my wounds just as Atlanta fell. And it was good I did, because Thomas' next mission required every cavalryman he could find. He had always wanted to have his own army, one that he did not have to inherit from any other general that he would be compared to, an army that he would be in charge of without reporting to another general on the scene. He got it after Atlanta.

We still had not defeated the Southern army, either in the east under Lee or in the west, now under Beauregard, who swung Hood's forty thousand men back to Alabama and straight up toward Nashville. Thomas could see what they were probably planning: a run through Tennessee, capturing Kentucky, and invading the north, across the Ohio River. If the Rebels were going to have to give up their cities, Chattanooga, Knoxville, Atlanta, even Richmond, then their last hope would be to offset those losses by threatening the northern countryside. Sherman and Grant knew where Hood was, but they thought he was only after lines of supply and communication. It was Forrest in middle Tennessee that worried them more. So they dispatched Thomas, with twenty-five thousand men and five thousand cavalry back to Tennessee to put down Forrest. Unfortunately, those thirty thousand men were not the Army of the Cumberland.

Sherman was going to take Thomas' old army with him as he plowed through Georgia to the sea—sixty-five thousand soldiers who were not going to encounter any enemy! He gave Thomas only two divisions from the Army of the Cumberland, one from the 4th under Newton and one from the 14th under James Morgan.

Neither had commanded a division before. Schofield would be Thomas' field commander, a lackey for Grant and Sherman and a poor fighter by all accounts.

So Thomas got what he wanted, you see—an army of his own—but it came with dirt in his mouth. Not the Army he trained and was devoted to, but new men and new leaders whom he would have to train all over again. His greatest accomplishment in the war—his most amazing feat—was what he did with those men that Sherman condescended to give him when Hood turned north and headed for Nashville.

Before that, he had to part with the army he led for three years, through Mill Springs, Perryville, Stone River, Chickamauga, Chattanooga, Kennesaw Mountain, Peachtree Creek, and countless lesser battles. Going back to Tennessee seemed like a retreat to him. (At least his men were spared that embarrassment.) After the war he would refuse all the palatial homes and large purses other generals were receiving from grateful citizens, and insist they be given to soldiers' relief funds. He would live on his governmental pay.

On September 26th he made his final rounds among the soldiers with whom he shared every danger. I will never, as long as I live, forget that day.

His aides alerted the generals who had been with him from the beginning that he was coming at nine a.m. All sixty thousand men—I mean every soldier, white and Negro—had his breakfast behind him, his boots polished, and his clothes pressed as best he could on a hot fall day in Georgia. The entire camp, just outside Atlanta, stood at attention as Thomas approached—"Old Slow Trot" they had always called him. This time no one thought the slow trot was funny. The generals that were still with him from the beginning stood in a line in front of the makeshift flagpole at the center of the circular camp: David

Stanley, Tom Wood, George Wagner, Bill Hazen, Sam Beatty, C.G. Harker, William Grose, all from the 4th Corp, and Morgan from the 14th—they had all been there since Mill Springs; Absalom Baird and John Turchin from the 14th and Henry Slocum from the 20th had fought with him since Stone River; and countless colonels had stayed throughout, without promotion. These men were backed by the generals and colonels who were newer to the ranks of the 4th, 14th, and 20th. And they were surrounded in the circle by rank after rank of the captains, lieutenants, sergeants, and privates that made the Army of the Cumberland so strong. The generals used to joke about George Thomas' knowing their sergeants' names better than they did. I knew from Stone River what they meant.

When we reached the outer rim of the circle, at least a half mile from its center, I dismounted and walked behind the general's horse; so did his aides. He stayed on Ashes, the gray mare that had been with him for three years, paused for a moment, and moved slowly forward, piercing the ring as an avenue opened up. As he passed, all soldiers turned toward him and saluted. And after he passed, the ranks closed behind those of us walking, and tightened.

Halfway in, he took off his hat and rested it on his hip.

Slowly, we moved closer and closer to the center. The center of the ring must have been fifty yards across; it was not until he emerged from the mass of troops and rode into that ring that he realized who was waiting for him there, that in front of the flag he loved were the officers who had been with him the longest. He stopped. I could see him slump ever so slightly, then straighten himself to a greater height than before. He slowly dismounted. You could hear your own breathing.

General Stanley stepped up on a small platform behind him, and beckoned General Thomas to walk forward. I slipped around the ring to where my own officers were located; I wanted to see Thomas' face and hear his words.

When General Thomas reached the foot of the platform, Stanley raised his arm to get everyone's attention. The silence was immediate.

"Members of the Army of the Cumberland, the greatest fighting unit in the United States Army." There was applause and hurrahs, but sudden quiet. "You all know why we are gathered here today." I looked over the endless crowd and could see Stanley's words translated backwards, row upon row, in every direction. He spoke deliberately to allow the words to be passed along.

"We are here to honor our leader, whom few of us will have the opportunity to follow to his future destiny.

"We, perhaps especially those of us who have know him for the entire war, want to acknowledge what he has done for us and our nation. Who knows what the future will bring in the months ahead. We may never see him again—fate may have other plans in store for all of us.

"Perhaps it is fitting that we must part from him before this war that has divided this country is over. It is fitting because we can bid goodbye to him when we are at our best, our most victorious. When we know in our hearts that our side is going to win.

"General, in the ordeal of this terrible war that has threatened to end the experiment that is the United States, you have bound us together in pride. You have trained us—without mercy—to fight as well as men can. You have shared all of our sorrows, never seeking for yourself privileges that you would not wish for us. General Thomas, we are what you have made us, and we wish only to give you back ourselves, alive or dead, in the spirit in which you gave yourself to us. All of us, every one of us, thanks you."

Every word seemed to swim through the air on heat waves to the outer reaches of the campground. General Thomas never for a moment took his eyes off David Stanley; tall as the general was, Stanley on the platform still towered over him. When Stanley had finished his oration, perfectly worded, he beckoned General Thomas to the platform as he simultaneously descended.

His innate shyness made the general uncomfortable with impromptu speeches. But, for once, he had no choice at all. And to his credit he did not hesitate for a moment.

When he stood on the platform, he gradually pivoted in a circle surveying his entire army. He stopped at the end of the circle when he came face to face with the officers who had been with him the longest. He began by talking directly to them, but soon enough his head raised and his eyes fixed on the farthest reaches of the assembled troops.

"My fellow soldiers," he began in his Southern drawl, "I am no public speaker. But I must be on this occasion. Some of you know that I have always wanted to have an army of my own, beholden to no one but me. Now they have given me that opportunity, but, sadly, it will include very few of you. It is not as I wanted it. I would rather stay here.

"I know so many of you that I will miss in person, to talk to, to encourage. But what I will miss most of all is how you carry yourself when the crisis comes, as it always does. If you have given me nothing else, it has been the way you handle the worst of times, not the best of times. The way you conduct yourself in the midst of battle, so honorably and courageously. No general has been more rewarded by his men than you have rewarded me. No general has been more blessed than I. You held your country in your hands, and your country is proud. Thank you, my men."

And as he finished, he doffed his hat and, ever so slightly, bowed his head.

A tumultuous roar simultaneously rose from all directions. It was not wild, or uncontrolled. It rolled across the campground and back again. Their hats were doffed in reply.

As General Thomas descended the two steps to the dirt below, with his head up, I stepped onto the platform: I had to see the expanse of men and what they would do when he finished.

The generals closest to him, without an audible sound, encircled him and closed in. Each in turn embraced him and said something in his ear.

But what was most amazing, which I cannot do justice to, was what happened then. Thousands of men all moved slowly toward where Thomas stood; the space at the center of the camp was soon gone. And as each general in front embraced him, he stepped to the side and let the man behind him move forward. Colonels followed generals. Colonels stepped aside and were followed by lieutenants. Lieutenants stepped aside and were followed by sergeants. On that September day, an hour after General Thomas had spoken, sergeants were stepping aside and even privates were coming forward, looking him in the eye, putting a hand on his shoulder, shaking his hand. And for another three hours, with no break in their gradual movement inward, the least of his men came forward. He never tired, never looked away from the eyes in front of him. He never lost composure, yet you knew that this was the most unforgettable moment of his life and that he was not going to miss one second of it. I never left the platform the entire time.

At last, when the throng had diminished, Thomas embraced the private before him—whoever he was—and made him the representative of all who had come before. He said, steadily, "Thank you for all you have done, son."

He stayed in place as his soldiers moved away. Then, a minute or two later, he turned to face me on the platform, and said, very quietly, "Are you not going to step forward, Colonel Swain? Are you just observing this, like a newspaperman?" He paused, then smiled. "It is all right, we will say our goodbyes later, William," and, as he turned back to Ashes, "I am looking forward to it."

did see him again, but my regiment was ordered to stay with Sherman, not Thomas, and I did not know if I would ever see the general after he left for Tennessee. Sherman wanted cavalry to handle the minor skirmishes his forces would encounter on the way to the coast, while his regular troops made the South "feel that war and individual ruin are synonymous," as he put it to Thomas. But we more or less sat around Atlanta for six weeks, unable to head across Georgia. I think Grant was not convinced that Hood could be defeated by Thomas if he ever turned north. Of course, Sherman did not want to chase Hood around Georgia and Alabama, so it took at least a month of his half-hearted engagements with Hood to persuade his superiors that they might as well let Sherman head east and leave a wake of destruction in his path. Sherman knew how good Thomas was, so he had no trouble convincing Grant of his own sincerity.

Before Sherman started east from Atlanta in early November, and long after Thomas had arrived in Nashville and sent out his infantry fruitlessly to track down Forrest and his marauding cavalry, Sherman called Newton's and Morgan's divisions back, along with five thousand new volunteers that Thomas had raised; in return, Thomas would finally get one of his old Corps from the Army of the Cumberland, not the 14th that he had commanded himself from '61 to '63, but the 4th Corp under Stanley. So my men and I did get to go north after all to be with the general. But we went without enough horses! Sherman kept most of them and left it to Thomas to find fresh mounts for the five thousand cavalry he inherited. General Schofield arrived, too, and assumed field command over his corps and Stanley's. (Thomas had not learned to distrust Schofield. He would learn soon enough.)

By the middle of November, several things were clear. General Thomas was going to have to defeat Hood alone, with no help from Sherman. Hood's army outnumbered Thomas', not even counting the thousands of cavalry under Forrest that were making havoc of one Union outpost after another from Murfreesboro to Mississippi. Thomas had to find far more men and train them to fight in short order, and he had to find thousands of horses for his cavalry or Forrest would have a clear road to the Ohio River, a path that Hood could follow if he was not intercepted. Hood was still in Alabama, on the other side of the Tennessee River; but the Union troops watching him, under Stanley and Schofield, were no match if he pressed north. I was there. I could see how numerous the Rebels were. Thomas' best hope was to fortify Nashville to the hilt and hope that Hood would take the bait and make the long march to attack, giving Thomas barely time to muster enough men to man the entrenchments he was madly digging around the city, into the rock ledge it was built on above the Cumberland River. Even the city's cemeteries had trenches winding among their silent citizens.

That November it poured and snowed on Tennessee day after day. The twenty-three thousand of us with Schofield began retreating, night and day, ahead of Hood. It was a muddy race to Nashville, one in which we had hardly any cavalry to counter Forrest's sorties. Maybe the only thing we had in our favor was the sorry condition of those Rebel troops; when we would capture them, they would have no shoes or coats. They were desperate. Hood had convinced them that the fate of the South was in their hands and only their hands. Hood himself had already lost an arm and a leg in the war, and sat like a scarecrow balanced on his horse. Every once in a while, when I reconnoitered for Stanley, I would catch a glimpse of the Confederate general. Only that man, I knew, could be leading these troops.

We just made it across the Duck River at Columbia, forty-five miles south of Nashville. We were rushing backwards, but it did not compare to the night march we made after that crossing. I learned later that Thomas ordered Schofield to move quicker, that he feared Hood had begun a turning movement to cut off his retreat. So Schofield left Stanley's 4th Corp behind at Spring Hill to cover the thousands of supply wagons that were jamming the road behind us. I knew we were in trouble.

As we passed through Spring Hill in the dead of night, the rain coming down, we could see hundreds of campfires not more than a half mile to the east. It had to be Rebels, and an army of them. We crept, wagons and all, alongside a mile of the enemy. "Like treading on ice covering a smoldering volcano," General Stanley put it. In four hours, till five in the morning, we moved ten thousand wagons and half again as many men around the drunk and sleeping Rebels. By the next night, November 29th, we reached Schofield and were fortifying Franklin, Tennessee, only fifteen miles from Nashville.

General Hood must have been furious when he found out what his men had done, or not done. He had sent them ahead, and they had missed their chance. Thomas could never have stopped Hood's invasion of Ohio and Indiana if Stanley had been caught in a surprise attack, trudging up the Pike to Nashville.

The very next night Hood sent those sleeping troops against our fortifications at Franklin, not waiting for his other corps to arrive from Alabama. Wave after wave of Rebels charged the entrenchments. The worst kind of horror reigned. Bodies of falling Rebels were six and seven deep in the trenches. We could hardly move to shoot the next wave coming over the top. Some of the dead were wedged standing up, as if they were carrying on conversations with us as we reloaded our guns. General Stanley took charge of the battle, furious that Schofield had stationed himself with a reserve division two miles away after positioning the front lines with their backs to the Harpeth River. It was one of Stanley's colonels who finally led the bayonet charge that put an end to the Rebel attacks. Stanley himself fell wounded, as did Forrest on their side. But the Rebels lost three times the number of men we lost, including at least a dozen generals and colonels waving their men forward.

We moved back to Nashville at dawn, leaving the gruesome scene to the surviving Confederates. I can only imagine what those soldiers must have thought when they saw their frozen comrades on the field of battle. They had seen dead before, over and over again, but no one on either side had ever seen so many from one side in one small place: upturned faces, disfigured or peaceful, that were sent to their death by a frantic general who had been embarrassed by his own officers' mistake.

George Thomas was still nervously pacing in Nashville. The thirty thousand men he brought up from the south would never hold against Hood; more had to be found. He called on Rosecrans of all people, who was commanding in Missouri, to send two divisions under A.J. Smith, but they were already a week overdue thanks to low water and Forrest's terrors in Western Tennessee. Thomas found five thousand quartermaster employees in Nashville and put them in charge of city defense. A combination of veterans of a hundred regiments, many having returned from voting in the North, soldiers just released from hospitals, and two brigades of Negro troops were united under General Steedman. The rest of the soldiers were newly conscripted men from the same farms above the Ohio River that gave me my regiment two years before—their youngest brothers and cousins. All these soldiers, with the 4th and 23rd Corps just arrived from Franklin, would comprise the mostly untested, unfamiliar troops that would confront Hood at Nashville. They equaled him in number but hardly in desperation or experience.

It would be up to George Thomas to get them ready. The one thing most needed was horses for the cavalry: Thomas ordered the seizure of every mule and horse in what was left of the farms of Kentucky and Tennessee, from the wealthy and poor alike. Even streetcar horses were commandeered. The circus lost all but the ponies that could not carry a soldier. It would only take Thomas a week to have the cavalry able enough to forestall Forrest and pursue Hood.

Grant could not wait. Sitting in Washington, he imagined that Hood was the confident pursuer and Thomas was on the defensive. In Grant's mind, no Northern general was as aggressive as himself and his protege, Bill Sherman. Never mind that Sherman avoided Hood and took off for Savannah, or that Thomas, as Grant himself feared, was not given enough men to defeat Hood if he went north. Thomas' plea to Grant—"It must be remembered that my command was made up of two of the weakest corps of General Sherman's army, and all the dismounted cavalry except one brigade"—fell on deaf ears. All Grant could imagine was that Forrest was about to cross the Ohio, Hood was charging forward, and Thomas was hunkering down in Nashville.

Telegrams flew. Starting on December 2nd, Grant wanted Thomas to attack at once, coming out of the entrenchments he had been building for weeks. Increasingly we were winning skirmishes in the area, even cavalry fights as more and more horses arrived, but Grant did not seem to get that news. By the 8th, Grant was threatening to replace Thomas, though there was no evidence that Hood had recovered from the Battle of Franklin. On the 9th an ice storm arrived and made footing impossible for man or beast; that very day Grant had decided to put Schofield in charge and drafted the order, later suspending it till the weather cleared. President Lincoln himself refused to endorse the move against his most successful general.

General Thomas saw what was happening, collected some of us in his headquarters and showed us copies of the dozens of telegrams that had gone back and forth between Grant and Halleck in Washington and himself in Nashville. I was there as second in command to James Wilson, the young general in charge of all of our cavalry. He defended Thomas' delays as essential for supplying the troops and giving them weather in which to operate. He had known Grant, too, at Vicksburg, and testified to his stubbornness. I would have added Grant's constant suspicion of Thomas, but I was the junior officer in the room. Only Schofield failed to openly support the necessary delays.

Thomas took me aside as the meeting broke up.

"Washington treats me like a boy, William, as if I cannot plan a campaign or fight a battle. If the weather thaws, I'll show them what will happen to Hood's army, unless I have completely misjudged the toll taken on his men by the march from Alabama and the battle at Franklin."

He wanted, finally, to have a conflict in the West that would be decisive, not another waste of human life in a hollow victory that allowed the Confederate army to move to another location. General Thomas had been in Nashville two years before, and now he was back again, with the war no closer to conclusion. But he had the Confederate army in the West where he wanted it: tied to their supply lines to the South and desperately in need of a base in Nashville to launch their invasion of Kentucky, and eventually the North. They would come to him.

But more telegrams came daily from Grant insisting on attack. Hood could not move either, of course, but that did not seem to matter. When December 13th arrived, ice still on the ground, Thomas wondered aloud why Grant with one hundred thousand men could not attack Lee in seven months, but could badger Thomas to attack a Confederate army that Sherman could not defeat with twice as many men as Thomas now had.

His mood was deepening.

He had finally begun to suspect someone in his midst of undermining his authority in Washington. When Steedman discovered it was Schofield's own telegrams to Grant, General Thomas could not understand why. "Who is next in command, General?" was Steedman's reply.

At last, that same afternoon, the thaw began and Thomas' spirits lifted. He had us all ready for battle at five a.m. a day later.

He was always ready. It was going to be his greatest victory.

And ours.

"We are going home, we are going home,
To die no more...."

the men sang before fires and lanterns were extinguished in the cold. They, too, sensed that something final was about to occur.

The cavalry—Wilson's nine thousand, including my regiment, are the key. Thomas has decided that we will circle the left flank of Hood's army on the outskirts of Nashville after our own left flank pretends to be the main attack. Our success, he tells us, will determine the outcome.

When the fog begins to lift on December 15th, Hood's forces gradually become visible behind a long stone wall on Montgomery Hill. The feint on our left is led by the Negro troops under Steedman's command, and they push beyond expectations, at great loss of life, forcing Hood to shift divisions from his center to his right. It is more than Thomas wants. With the sound of a bugle, Wilson waves us forward through barren, muddy fields. We are at the opposite end of the line from our Negro troops. But we are not mounted. Our horses are held in the rear for that moment when the Rebels run and have to be pursued—General Thomas is that confident.

At eight o'clock we begin to move, and I look back and catch a glimpse of him, finally wearing his Major General of Volunteers' uniform. He never wore a new uniform till long after his last promotion; but he always picked an important moment to put it on. Only his gold braid stands out in the fog.

We are trotting forward over desolate fields. Pockets of fog arise like smoke and obscure our view of the hills ahead. At the beginning we are not as close to the Rebels as Steedman is on the left; it is as if Thomas wants us to get a running start before we see them. Forrest's cavalry are supposed to be there, we expect them. But all we see are a few hundred men on horse, exposed to our repeating rifles. It is Forrest's men all right, I can tell by the colors they carry. But there are so few of them! They scatter as we push forward.

Montgomery Hill comes into view, but much farther to our left than the men expect. It becomes clear that Wilson's task is to circle the hill and the stone wall and the enemy.

We are scared. Not a one of us had ever been there, behind enemy lines. It must be like our own, a hodgepodge of many things, artillery and supply wagons, reserve troops standing still, their guns at rest, or milling about and saying their good-byes to men in other regiments. Men praying. Others paying no attention to anything.

How could we get behind Hood at the start of a battle? Thomas must have known exactly what had happened to Hood since he left Alabama—he did not have enough men to reach to the outer edges of Thomas' own army. That is why Thomas would take anyone in Nashville who would shoulder a gun! If he was going to attack and put Hood on the defensive, then he would have the ability to spread his men out more than Hood. If Hood attacked, the opposite might have been true.

So Thomas knew all along that he was going to attack. He was drawing Hood toward an attack on himself!

As we swing around the west end of the Hill, Wood and Smith and Schofield send their men against the wall nearest us, halfway up the hill. Three corps against one, the odds are in our favor. Steedman must be holding at least two corps in place. The fog and smoke from the rifles are indistinguishable, except for the smell of gunpowder. The rattle of musketry is deafening.

We are the ones who meet the Rebel corps held in reserve. They are not ready at all. There is a rise we must go up, too. We are shooting and reloading the whole time, but the Confederates behind the front lines seem so startled they do not know what to do. They cannot run to the rear, they are already there, and the wagons block their way. They are not in proper formation to counter our gradual ascent. They fight, but they fight as individual men, not brigades. And their aim is bad, they do not act like they understand the point of returning our fire. It seems as if no one has ever told them that this kind of attack might ever happen.

What they finally do, as Wood's men overrun the wall, is mix with the Rebels who really are retreating and all of them begin sliding down the line away from us toward the center of the Hill, where Hood's army has not yet been engaged. By four-thirty the sun is setting on the strangest battle I have ever been in: Thomas' strategy has been perfect, almost as if he knew exactly where every one of Hood's men was going to be and how to break his spirit.

Some of us mount to reconnoiter as the artillery dies in the night. Sweeping again to the right through the woods, we can look to our left and see across the fields, a half mile at a time, roads to the south packed with retreating soldiers. They are not even running, just slogging along, steady, together. Only when they reach Shy's Hill, two miles down the way, do they stop and turn. Their colonels and then generals arrive to form them into lines and dig the trenches for another fight. We ride back with the news of what to expect on the morrow. But before we reach our own camp, already moving to the south as well, we pass pockets of hundreds of butternut prisoners, their heads down, ashamed no doubt of the day's events. Whole brigades will have to be detached just to guard those captured. They use the excavation for the capitol building in Nashville to hold a thousand of them.

Forrest and his cavalry were nowhere to be seen. My division and the rest of Wilson's nine thousand had been a feeble, ill-equipped band of five thousand strangers a month before. Somehow Thomas had put us in position to embarrass the greatest cavalry leader in the war. Forrest was the worst son of a bitch there was, a ruthless lover of slavery, but he was the best fighter the Confederates had. And he was gone when they needed him most. General Wilson and I wondered how Thomas knew that, as he must have, and we did not.

During the night we move closer and closer to Hood's positions. We do not change any of our own. I am still way out on the right flank, Smith and Schofield next. But at dawn Thomas adds a new force: artillery. The end of Hood's line on Shy's Hill forms a salient, a loop, and the general realizes that it can be bombarded from two directions. His plan is still the same—turn Hood inward from our right, his left, and roll him into panic.

Again we circle, meeting some disorganized resistance. My men even capture an enemy courier with a message from Hood to the cavalry commander, Chalmers, who was sent to confront us: "For God's sake drive the Yankee cavalry from our left and rear, or all is lost." By noon we are in the rear of Hood's army. We are looking at the backs of the enemy! They know we are there, we are firing at them from eighty yards away, now on our horses, weaving in and out of the abandoned wagons and artillery. But they are being attacked from three sides and they cannot give their attention to only one.

Wood's men are forcing their way up the slope from the north, Smith from the west, and us in the south, gradually closing the net on Shy's Hill. I learn later that Schofield was hesitating to send his men up the slope as Wood had already done, and that General Wilson himself circled all the way back to Schofield's headquarters and made clear to Thomas that, sitting there behind Rebel lines, we are horribly exposed unless Schofield, or somebody, moves to link up with us on their right and Wood on their left. "My men are in Hood's rear," he yelled as he leaped off his horse. "You can see their guidons fluttering through the field glasses. For God's sake, get Schofield to attack." Thomas took one look through the glasses, saw Smith's Corps beginning to move forward, and, without even looking at Schofield, said, "You will attack at once." He does.

At that very moment, the Negro troops under Steedman's command are avenging their losses in the earlier assault and taking Overton Hill at the other end of Hood's line, a mile away. For the first time in this long war, white Southern troops are turning and running from Negro Federals. "This proves the manhood of the Negro," General Thomas tells us that night.

In that last hour of battle on December 16th, between three and four o'clock, as the first rays of sunset begin to appear, I witness something both glorious and horrible. I am there for the certain death of the Confederacy.

Up and down the line, the enemy disintegrates. Ranks break, divisions and brigades and regiments and companies lose their shape and existence. The shoeless, hopeless soldiers from the South become individuals again, never to reform or fight with any heart. Five thousand of them surrender. Twenty thousand more just leave the hill, stepping over their fallen comrades. The ones we capture are in tears; the ones leaving must be, too.

Now my men and I start our pursuit. General Thomas does not just want to win the Battle of Nashville. Why should I be surprised that he wants to destroy Hood's army as a fighting unit, and that means pursuit?

Our saddlebags are packed with rations, our repeating rifles—the envy of our army—are in hand. We shoot no one in the back, no one who does not resist. Ten days later and across the border into Georgia, we have captured eight thousand more prisoners. In the Battle of Nashville, the Rebels have lost three times the killed and wounded as we, but General Thomas has planned every move so well that their greatest losses are in the

Charge of the Cavalry

number captured and in their broken spirit. Only nine thousand of the fifty-five thousand men that Hood brought from Alabama have crossed the Tennessee River in return.

The first night, before Wilson and I lead our men south, he and I are scouting the Granny White Turnpike, a mile behind the retreating Rebels. We hear a lone horseman coming up fast, a messenger from the general, probably telling us to speed up. Not so.

"Is that you, Wilson? Hulloh, Bill!"

It is the general himself.

"Damn it to hell, I knew we could do it! I told Grant we could do it!"

He must see our astonished faces. He straightens up in the saddle.

"Follow them as far as you can tonight and resume the

pursuit as early as you can tomorrow morning."

He wheels on Ashes and disappears, like a ghost that brings good news, not bad.

❖-❖-❖

Two weeks after we pursued Hood all the way into Georgia, I saw General Thomas again, at his headquarters in Nashville. I had missed his authority and voice. We walked away from the city. It was one of those beautiful starlit nights when every soldier has thoughts of home and quiet evenings, of the thousand and one pleasant scenes in life. You could hear one of the regimental bands parading down a city street in the distance, probably infuriating Rebel sympathizers. I had never seen Thomas so reflective and calm.

"That campaign, William, went as well as it could have."

"I know, General, it was brilliant."

"I mean something more than intelligence and planning. For the first time, I felt that my abilities and my men's abilities were truly being used—by some force beyond myself. Is that sacrilegious, to talk of one side in war as part of some God-given plan? Those soldiers we fought and defeated and drove home to their families in rags are just as religious as you and I, some more so. It cannot be that God sides with either the North or the South. But I also cannot shake the feeling that something more than me and my soldiers was at work here."

We became pensive. We skirted the camp of the 4th Corps, what was left with Thomas of the Army of the Cumberland. The men were singing an Irish ballad that was hardly religious or patriotic:

'Twas a windy night, about two o'clock in the morning,
An Irish lad, so tight, all the wind and weather scorning,
At Judy Callahan's door, sitting upon the paling,
His love tale he did pour, and this is part of his wailing:
Only say you'll be mistress Brallaghan;
Don't say nay, charming Judy Callaghan.

Hundreds of voices picked up the chorus and repeated it. The men were relaxed and happy, as they should be. But their mood was not the same as the general's and mine. We walked on into the night.

"They want to give me the promotion to a regular Major General, William, the one I should have gotten long ago, after Chickamauga," his voice suddenly angry. "There is one thing about my promotions that is gratifying: I have never received one they dared to withhold."

We walked some more.

"Maybe you could look at it this way," I offered, "as their finally understanding your value to the country, truly understanding it. You have not been treated fairly, I know that. It has hurt me to see it. But you are different than they are, and a Southerner by birth: you expect too much if you want them to understand what makes you different than what they already know. So you did the only thing you could do, let the victories eventually make it impossible for them not to recognize you. Anyway, you have always had the recognition and admiration of your men and the American people. I am a newspaperman, remember."

He looked at me. "And a wise one at that. I should have told you that there is another promotion we can discuss. General Wilson has put you in for Brigadier General, and I have signed it and sent it on to the War Department. That means it will happen."

We stopped walking. I realized that I was facing him, looking him directly in the eye for a rare moment. I could not speak. I had never thought about my own recognition. But he had, and it meant the world to me.

. "You, too, had to wait a while, Bill. Perhaps we are more alike than you realized."

11

Neala and I had been writing twice a week for the past year. When I went into the hospital the second time, before Atlanta, it was her voice I would hear in my dreams; marriage could not come soon enough.

So I made my way back to Vernon again after Nashville, anticipating my new life as a husband and my return to the newspaper. The war would be over in three months, and my men and I would not see the likes of a real battle again.

Neala had organized a welcome home gathering at the town hall. I requested that all the area families of fallen soldiers be invited, so I could speak to them directly. Most of the town came, I think for some deeper understanding of the future.

The mayor gave a speech about our victories and officially welcomed me home, referring to me, for the first time, as General Swain, and remembering all who had fought and those who had given their lives to hold our union together. Pride and sorrow filled the air.

"Thank you," I said, "for your warm reception. All of us,

at home and on the battlefield, have sacrificed much for the sake of our country. The war's deepest purpose was to fight for this country's beliefs and to keep our democracy secure. Our forefathers set in motion a great experiment in freedom. It will be challenged again and again, but we will continue to remember the true meaning of their words and fight whenever necessary. What is most important is our commitment to all our citizens, because the individual is never as great as the whole.

"Our task now is to learn from this experience. What General Thomas taught me is that being alive means living with contradictions. The Bible says to love ourselves and our neighbors, but we sometimes do the opposite, out of fear, out of ignorance, and often in war, out of necessity. In the face of that, we must always be mindful of the legacy we are leaving for generations to come: understanding and forgiveness of our enemies, fearlessness in defense of our principles, and faith that, as we strive toward greater awareness, it is God's will. I speak for all those boys, here and gone, who have understood that legacy. We are so grateful for their sacrifice."

The crowd was quiet and appreciative. The rest of the evening was spent comforting each other.

Four months later, after my men and I were mustered out in Washington, DC, Neala and I were married. It was September 9, 1865, and my new life was just beginning. Over the next twenty-five years, I remained the owner and editor of the *Vernon Banner*. We had great happiness and great sorrow—two of our five children died of childhood diseases, but the other three, a boy and two girls, grew to adulthood and made us proud. Our son George now works with me, as editor of the paper. Neala strives tirelessly for women's suffrage, and has remained the strong, independent partner I loved and admired so much. One of my greatest joys is the knowledge that we hold each other in such high esteem.

12

We remained in contact with the general and Frances Thomas, and saw them for the last time in 1869 when they were traveling from Louisville to San Francisco for his final military post. He had spent four years commanding the Military District of the Tennessee, including Kentucky, Mississippi, Alabama, and Georgia, successfully persuading Tennessee to return to the Union and ratify the 14th Amendment to the Constitution that gave citizenship to American Negroes. He arranged for pardons of former Confederate officers, but was also the first leader to warn the government in Washington about the organization of the Ku Klux Klan, under Nathan Bedford Forrest, in Nashville in 1867. Though he refused to run for President against Grant, he obviously had true political skills, and Tennessee gave him, the Northern general who overwhelmed the South at Nashville, a special citizenship to their state. You can imagine what this meant to the man who was disowned by his own Southern state. When he and General Hood met by chance in Louisville, Thomas comforted his crippled rival. Later, Hood said, "Thomas is a grand man. He should have remained with us, where he would have been appreciated and loved."

Before he and Frances came to Vernon that last time, I went to Cincinnati to see him when he was elected the first president of the Society of the Army of the Cumberland in 1868. Grant and Sherman were there and, to their chagrin, heard his acceptance speech and the endless applause that followed. It concluded with these words:

> We have not only broken down one of the most formidable rebellions that ever threatened the existence of any country, but the discipline of the Army of the Cumberland alone has civilized two hundred thousand patriots and citizens. I have traveled a little since the war was over. Wherever I have been, whether on steamboat or rail, I have either seen on the steamboat, engaged in peaceful occupation of merchant sailors, or I have seen in the fields, along the railroads, engaged in peacefully following the plough, and setting an example of industry worthy to be followed by all the country, men innumerable dressed in blue. They did not disdain to wear the uniform; they gloried in it; and I hope that such sentiments, and such civilizing influences as have been produced by this war, will serve for all time to inspire this nation with such a feeling of patriotism that no enemy can ever do us the least harm.

We named our first child after George Henry Thomas, and he was pleased to meet his namesake on that last visit with Frances. He held my three-year old boy at eye level and said, "I am George Henry Thomas. What is your name?" "That is my name, too!" Georgie exclaimed. "You have the same name as me!" As he lowered him to the floor, the general told him that I had been a great soldier in the war. "I am going to be a great soldier, too," Georgie answered. "Well, that's wonderful, son. War is a great challenge, but always remember that there are things worth fighting for, you just have to decide what those things are." "What's 'challenge' mean, sir?" With that the general let out a great laugh and settled into an enjoyable evening that reminded me of our wonderful dinner in Chattanooga. He and Frances remained devoted to one another to the end. I always felt that his military assignment to San Francisco was another penalty for being a Southerner who loved his country too much for his own good.

❊ ❊ ❊

In March 1870, I received a cable from San Francisco in the *Banner* office. It was from J.P. Willard, the general's aide.

> GENERAL THOMAS DIED LAST NIGHTstopNATURAL CAUSESstopMEMORIAL SERVICE TOMORROWstopWILL BE BURIED IN TROYstopTRAIN LEAVING ON 31STstopWILL GO THROUGH INDIANAPOLISstopCAN YOU TAKE HIM WITH ME FROM INDIANA?stopREPLY LICK HOUSEstop
>
> J.P. WILLARD

Harper's Weekly later called it a "national calamity."

I cabled Willard that I would join the train in Indianapolis and accompany the body to Troy.

There was no way of knowing for sure what day it would reach Indiana, so I was in the capitol, on April 4th, a day before it could have arrived. By the next day, Indianapolis was teeming with mourners, and every hotel room was full.

People milled around outside, waiting for only one thing.

We had read that crowds had greeted the train in every city on the way east—fifty thousand in Chicago alone, I later read—but I had no idea they were as large as the one gathering in Indianapolis. It was a painful reunion, too: many of my old soldiers from other towns in Indiana were there and recognized me. They talked as if they had lost their best friend, his influence on their lives was so strong.

General Thomas had found a way, without friendship, to let them know that he valued each of their lives, that he did not want to do without any one of them. Winning a battle, so important to him, would be inevitably tarnished by any one of their deaths. Every man who died was an individual human being, without exception, older or younger, richer or poorer, white or Negro.

The train, only an engine and three cars, the middle car bedecked with American flags draped from the window sills, the only car with its lights on, slid slowly into the Indianapolis station in the evening of April 5th. Soldiers and citizens were peering inside, sometimes holding up their children for a view.

Willard waived me in as the train paused ever so briefly. No speeches were to be made; no ceremonies at each stop. All was solemn.

"How are you, General Swain? It is a sad day for all of us."

"I am fine, Willard. How is Mrs. Thomas? Will she accept my condolences tonight?"

"General, she is not on the train."

"Why on earth not?"

"She conducted the memorial service in San Francisco and stayed behind to take care of the general's private papers. She commissioned me to carry out her wishes in Troy."

"But why would she not accompany his body, she loved and honored him so much?"

"I can tell you this. President Grant and General Sherman both tried to persuade her to allow the general to be buried at West Point, where they all were in school together. She was angry that they would try to claim him in death when they had so little respect for his service in life. And she told them her decision in her wire East; I wrote it down as she instructed: 'I regret that I cannot yield to the desire of having the burial at West Point. As Troy will be my future home, I feel that I must bury General Thomas in my family plot at the cemetery there. I will leave to you the arrangements for a military funeral at Troy. Private services have already been held here. Frances L. Thomas.' But she was much angrier than that; so angry that to see them fawn over the general in front of the regular citizens who truly admired him, she said, would distress her too much. She had paid her respects in San Francisco. He would be waiting for her in Troy when she returned home."

Inside the car almost all the seats had been removed, except for two rows at each end facing each other. I sat in the nearest one, which looked down the length of the funeral car. Colonel Willard sat across from me, his back to the mammoth coffin where the aisle used to be. He did not need to see it again; he had been its only steady company for two thousand miles.

It was a mahogany coffin, dark in color, though you could not see much beyond the huge American flag that was lain over it and the ivy along its edges. No one else was in the car. We had gone from being immersed in a crowd of twenty thousand people fanning out from the train station, to the silence of the general's own presence.

The train picked up speed but never went fast, perhaps twenty miles an hour. When we cleared Indianapolis and began to reach the towns and farms that lay beyond, I looked out the window, through the reflection of the coffin in the glass, to see if

I could detect anything in the dark. Mile after mile after mile, you would see lanterns swinging next to the tracks, back from the tracks, a hundred yards away, across entire fields. Each lantern was held by an arm that extended in the dark to the face of a man or woman. Some heads were bowed while the lanterns swung. Most faces looked straight into the funeral car, solemnly.

No one could have spread the word so far to swing lanterns: it was the way of expressing themselves in the dark that they all chose, in town after town. How could you deny their symbol: George Henry Thomas had been their light in the dark. For at least an hour we looked out the window as we rode by the lanterns. Neither of us spoke, it seemed so mysterious. The only sound was the rattle of the train wheels on the tracks.

After a while I needed conversation to help me deal with the silence and grief in the car: "What are you able to tell me, Colonel, about his final days, and about Frances and the events in San Francisco?"

"Mrs. Thomas gave me explicit instructions to tell you everything that happened, no matter how long it takes. She believed that, of all people, you would want to know everything, with nothing bad or good omitted. But she wanted you to read this letter from her first, before I told you anything." And he handed the letter to me.

Dear William,

Colonel Willard will have explained to you already why I cannot be with you and my General on his journey to my family in Troy. He will tell you as well about my husband's death. I need to share with you things you do not already appreciate about George Thomas, things you need to know.

Our marriage was so important to him, even

though we would spend long periods apart. I remember our dinner in Chattanooga so vividly, and how much my husband trusted you.

He and I had an honesty that saw us through very lonely times, when we were apart and together. George believed in his soul that each person has a destiny to fulfill, but that only you can know your own destiny; and I discovered when I met him, and we would circle the bandstand late at night on the grounds of West Point, reading Hawthorne's stories to each other, that I believed it, too. If you find what you believe is your destiny, you must see it through, come what may. There will be setbacks all the time. You will be your own worst judge. But you will be measured by God, as I know I am, on how you kept your faith, not only in Him but in yourself. If we knew the other was doing what he was called to do, it was worthwhile, whatever the consequences. My husband died doing that.

He knew, my dear friend, that life is a working out of one's destiny, and that no one—except one's closest friends—can understand what passes between oneself and one's God. The worst pain is knowing that you can never be all that one's destiny requires. We can never be as forgiving as God. We are never more than human.

I cannot tell you, William, how much it means to me that you have boarded this train and will be with George until the end.

With my deepest gratitude,
Frances Kellogg Thomas

When I had finished the letter, Willard began his account of the general's death.

"We had finished the mapping project in California the week before, and he was looking forward to a rest. That same day an anonymous article from the *New York Tribune* reached him that claimed the Nashville campaign in 1864 was won at Franklin, not Nashville, and that Grant was right to want to remove the lumbering General Thomas from command. The general was hurt to the quick. He had only recently found out that Grant wanted to remove him; now it was being broadcast in an important newspaper. I am sure you can understand that, General Swain. He suspected that Schofield was behind it, if he did not actually write the article. I was certain of it. After dwelling on the unfairness and suddenness of the attack for a day, he sat down to write a reply. I do not know if you ever saw any of his battle reports, General, but they were meticulous and fair in their account of the fighting; his reply to the *Tribune* article was the same way: instead of unleashing his anger, he retold in minute detail the battles of Franklin and Nashville, with the right emphasis on General Stanley's and General Wilson's roles in comparison to Schofield.

"He never finished. Colonel Hough, his other aide, found him slumped on his desk, in and out of consciousness, his writing blurred and disconnected for the last few sentences. Hough helped him to the window for air, but the general fainted away. He regained consciousness a few minutes later, then complained of a pain in his temple and lay down again. Mrs. Thomas hurriedly arrived and sat by his side; she and Hough and I were the only ones in the room when he whispered a few words in her ear. I will never know what he said. He suddenly convulsed as if he was trying to rise.

"Doctors came, but he was unconscious by now, and all they could do was cup his temples. They said it was apoplexy. His pulse grew weaker as the hours passed. None of us left the room. A few other officers came in. Mrs. Thomas' sister, too. He was that way for five hours.

"Then, about seven-thirty in the evening, there was a last, little convulsion, and his breathing stopped.

"He lay in state the next day in their rooms at Lick House. We had a private Episcopal service right there two days after he died; Mrs. Thomas wanted the military funeral somewhere else. The military had made him rise, she said, and it made him fall.

"Naturally the flags in San Francisco flew at half staff. Law courts adjourned, and buildings were draped in black. By the following day, we had put his coffin on a train in Oakland after a ferry ride from San Francisco. Guns sounded for fifty-three minutes from Alcatraz Island as the ferry made its way across the bay to Oakland. He was fifty-three when he died."

"You know, I was General Thomas' aide for a long time, in the war and afterward. This trip across the country is a testimony to his leadership. If he had to die, William, I am glad it was in San Francisco, because it meant that everyone has had a chance to say goodbye to him. Mrs. Thomas and I made all the transportation arrangements, a change of military details in Utah and Nebraska and Illinois and Ohio, ferrying the funeral car across the Mississippi River and hooking it to a second train waiting in East St. Louis, planning its route to New York. Even when the Mississippi was too high to carry the original car, we had an emergency plan to remodel a car on the second train, the one we are in now, and just ferry his body across. Riding alone on that boat with his body across the Mississippi was unforgettable. We left one crowd on one shore and were in the hands of nature before we joined another crowd on the Illinois side; it took a long time, the Mississippi is a half mile wide at that point. I was more frightened than in any battle with him. He needed me to protect him for once, not the other way around. I never took my hand off the coffin, as if I could carry it the rest of the way if the ferry capsized.

"The new railroad car was waiting when we got there. We made up some time till now, and we will get to Schenectady on schedule."

"But I have still omitted the most important moments on the trip. They had nothing to do with me. You saw swinging lanterns in Indiana, and we'll probably see more to come. When we slow in stations, we hear the tolling bells and military salvos, and flowers are put on the train at every entrance. You could see and hear that in Indianapolis. That has been true everywhere.

"It is dark now, but at dawn I think you will see something else that has been true since we left Oakland, California. I saw it in Utah and Wyoming and Nebraska and Missouri. We will see it in Ohio and New York, too."

He paused for a breath.

"They build arches over the tracks. Not overpasses that are already there, new arches. Arches of flowers from all parts of the country. The train passes slowly through them. And on those arches of flowers they have spelled out in silver and gold, repeatedly, the names of General Thomas' victories. Mill Springs, Perryville, Stone River, Chattanooga, Franklin, Nashville. And they have arches for Chickamauga, William, for Chickamauga! That was not a victory! It is as if the people know how he felt about that battle, that he was as proud of us that day as he was at Chattanooga or Nashville. The people know him, they do.

"I will never forget those arches as long as I live. They say everything anyone needs to know about the general's contribution to his country, and how it is appreciated."

As the sorrow engulfed us, we could only sleep fitfully in that lighted car for a few hours, until the Ohio dawn woke us up. I rose first and quietly walked back through the last car on the train.

The detail of soldiers that half-filled the car were still asleep.

When I opened the rear door and stepped onto the platform, the car passed under an arch of flowers. Soldiers in uniform, white and Negro alike, surrounded by crowds on both sides of the tracks, saluted the general.

The arch read "CHICKAMAUGA."

I saluted in return until they were out of sight.

13

We reached Schenectady in the early morning of April 7th. Colonel Willard asked me to deal with any dignitaries who were there, while he checked the arrangements for transporting the body to Troy. The very last person I wanted to see, General Schofield, was waiting to receive General Thomas. Short in stature, with his long beard and balding head, and not even forty years old, he repulsed me. How could I deal with him, knowing what I knew about the general's death and all that had gone before? This was what Frances wanted to be spared.

Schofield did not remember my name, of course, but he recognized my rank and my status in the funeral car. He explained with polite indifference that President Grant was waiting with his other cabinet members in Troy, and that he was to accompany the body the twenty miles to the memorial service at St. Paul's Episcopal Church. I could see he was looking for Mrs. Thomas but did not have the courage to ask where she was. I was silent.

I deferred to Schofield but insisted on riding in the carriage with him. The Colonel signaled that the arrangements were satisfactory, everything was as expected, and the cortege moved down the hill onto the main street in Schenectady and up the rise toward Albany. Schofield spent the entire ride trying every few minutes to make conversation. I was not going to give him that satisfaction. I wanted him to feel my disdain.

It was a tedious ride, though crowds of people lined the roads, saluting and waving American flags. When I learned that Schofield was going to be one of the pallbearers, I gave up any feeling that I could control the events that were about to transpire. Grant and Sherman would do things the way they wanted to do them; I could only hope that the people themselves—the ordinary soldiers and citizens, and the officers who served under Thomas—would make their presence known. It was a relief to know that Generals Hazen and Granger and Newton, all admirers of the general, were going to be pallbearers, too.

It took a full five hours to navigate the distance to the church. There, the men from Oakwood Cemetery on the bluff across from St. Paul's carefully unloaded the coffin and transported it inside the church to lie in state until the following morning. Even then, the day before the service and before visitors were allowed, hundreds of people stood outside in the crisp Spring air, trying to get a glimpse of a soldier they felt some personal allegiance to.

I walked the three blocks to the hotel where the colonel had made my reservation. Before going up to my room I read an editorial I had brought with me from the *Chicago Tribune* that I wished I had written:

> In General Thomas there seemed to be a union of all the qualities which make up the great and successful soldier. He brought no peculiar trait of character into stronger relief than any other, but blended them all in perfect harmony. Although a Virginian by birth, he was a

staunch, uncompromising Unionist in feeling. As a soldier, he united skillful strategy with cool valor and tremendous power. When he fought, he hurled all his forces upon the enemy and crushed him. He was as distinguished in council as he was terrible in battle. As a gentleman, he was irreproachable, both in contact with his men and with the world, and none ever loved more dearly this lion-heart with the affections of a woman, than his own soldiers who served under him and knew the warm feelings under the stern exterior. As a man, he was manly in all things. Not a spot of meanness or jealousy stain his long and useful career. In his personal appearance, he was dignified and commanding; in his bearing, gentle and courteous, and in his habits strictly temperate and rigid. His fame is forever assured in the history of his country, and his life is a model for the emulation of every Christian soldier and every aspiring youth in America.

The memorial service the next day was at eleven in the morning, and Colonel Willard came for me at ten. We went through the front doors of the hotel and were immediately engulfed in a sea of people. I had a hard time even keeping an eye on Willard as he pushed ahead. Endless people, soldiers and civilians, for three solid blocks, right up to the steps of the church: it took us at least thirty minutes to get there.

Once inside it was easier navigating, though hundreds of people, without designated pews, were already standing in the back. I was assigned to the third row and Willard went ahead to the front row as Mrs. Thomas' representative.

The coffin was on a dais in front of the chancel, and four

ministers sat behind, two on the left of the altar and two on the right. The whole church was draped in flowers. Your eye went from one garland to the next. The immortelles and ivy that had been twined around the casket in California were still in place. An elegant crown of evergreens and roses, with a cross of immortelles, was at its head, a wreath of japonicas and lilies at its foot. A plain silver plaque on the coffin bore the simple inscription: "General George Henry Thomas, U.S. Army. Born July 31, 1816. Died March 28, 1870." President Grant and General Sherman and General Sheridan sat stiffly in the front pew, looking past the coffin and its flowers.

The pastor at the Episcopal church, a Reverend Bishop Doane, conducted the ceremony. He spoke briefly about the general's military career, then concentrated, in words I remember, on the effect he had on his men:

> "Silent, sedate, never familiar, though always kind, he had none of the petty arts and practiced none of the stage devices that sometimes attract a short-lived popularity. He had never tolerated the slightest evasion of duty, from his brigadiers down to his orderlies. Always, when possible opportunity was afforded, he had visited the regimental hospitals and looked himself after the condition of the sick. Many a hospital steward in the old Cumberland Army remembers the unexpected and personal inspection which the sick-quarters received from the Major General himself. He was a man who made no distinctions among men."

I looked over at Grant and Sherman again, wondering if they understood any of this. They were immovable, respectful, stiff. They must have been relieved that they had no angry wife to console in the pew across from them, and no eulogy at her request to give from the pulpit. And there was not a single member of the Thomas family in the church; a whole pew was empty for them in the second row. The general was alone with his colleagues, those that loved him and those that were frightened by him. Grant and Sherman remained stoic as long as they were in military company, persuaded, I was sure, that they had somehow done a better job than Thomas. After all, they had won the war.

The reverend said something else:

"He is home now. I do not mean in Troy, New York, far from his home of origin. I mean in our hearts. Our thanks to the Kellogg family and his wife, Frances, who has already said her good-byes to the husband she loved, I came to know General Thomas. He was a man without a home. Not in Virginia, not in Tennessee where his soldiers shed their blood, not in San Francisco, not anywhere with a family. The closest he came was here, and here he will be buried. We must be his family and carry on his spirit. We must take him to our hearts as our patriarch. We here today must represent the America that was his true family."

Amen, I thought.

❦❦❦

At the end of the service, the pallbearers came forward, lifted the coffin, and moved slowly toward the back of the church. Granger and the others who fought with Thomas had been moved to tears, except Schofield, of course, whose face was rigid and impassive. Maybe his participation was some strange kind of justice for Thomas. The pallbearers moved in unison as if they had done this many times before. The front pews filed in behind them for the walk down the steps and the ascent up the hill across the street into Oakwood Cemetery.

But the bearers could not carry it up the hill, which was too steep. A wagon drawn by horses was waiting at its foot, and as they slid it gently into place and the driver gently spurred the horses forward and up the tree lined path, I looked down the street for the first time. And I could not see the street at all in either direction; there were people everywhere, soldiers mixed with civilians, old and young, men and women, Negro and white.

Standing not twenty feet from me was General Brannan, in charge of the regular army regiments at the funeral. He was saluting as the coffin passed, but looked me straight in the eye. He recognized me if Schofield did not. All he said, quietly and only to me, was, "We know what is true and what is not, William, don't we?"

Yes, we did. And the people did, too.

It took a long time to reach the gravesite. We were trudging not very far behind the wagon holding the casket, and every once in a while, when the path wound to the left or the right, I looked back down the hill at the crowd following us. Leaves were still waiting to appear on the trees, so I never lost sight of the street and the church. The path kept filling with regiments and ordinary people in some kind or order. But the street never emptied. It was like a sponge drawing more and more Americans to the bottom of the hill.

It took us at least twenty minutes just to reach the crest. Oakwood was one of those new cemeteries that were put around nature, around the trees and hills, instead of making the area flat for graves. If I had closed my eyes and only thought of the world I was walking through, it would have felt like a Sunday stroll. Maybe that was the point, to make death seem less frightening.

Over the crest it was another hundred yards to the gravesite, down a second path and left at a third. Mausoleums began to appear, grand like miniature granite houses with pillars and doorways. Or tall monuments to town leaders or generals in one war or another. Lesser monuments for other family members, even some modest gravestones, circled the tall ones. Then trees or a hillock would interrupt and you would forget for a moment that you were in a cemetery.

The wagon reached the site. No one was in any hurry. The eight pallbearers, all generals, assembled and slowly removed the casket. They settled it on their shoulders and walked carefully into the Kellogg family plot that stretched fifty feet on each side. Frances' father and mother were buried under what looked like a little Washington Monument. Three of their sons who had died before reaching the age of fifty were buried with them. And thirty feet away, to the left, was the family vault that would hold his remains until his own monument could be completed.

I already knew what it was going to look like from what Colonel Willard had told me of Frances' wishes. It was not big, perhaps seven feet high and ten feet wide, a solid granite sarcophagus with an American eagle mounted on top grasping a sword like the one he carried in the war or the gilded one his family refused to send to the funeral. On the front, in modest letters, it said: George H. Thomas, Major-General U.S.A. Born in Southampton County, Virginia. July 31, 1816 Died, San Francisco, Cal. March 28, 1870. It was heavy looking, like the general, but it was modest compared to other monuments in Oakwood. And it would be surrounded by the only family that still loved him and would protect his memory. Frances was to be buried next to him, under the same eagle.

The pallbearers set the coffin down on a makeshift platform next to the vault until everyone had reached the top of the hill and assembled down the third path.

It took an hour and a half!

An army band, fifty yards away, played "Rock of Ages" and "Lead us, O Father, in the Paths of Peace."

Every knoll and hillock, every swale in this beautiful cemetery, was filled with people.

President Grant, Generals Sherman and Sheridan, and a dozen other dignitaries stood at the edge of the Kellogg plot; it was as if they were not allowed further, no matter what their rank. All of us bowed heads as the minister read the burial service:

> Thou only are immortal, the creator and maker of mankind; and we are mortal, formed of the earth, and unto earth shall we return. For so thou didst ordain when thou createdst me, saying, 'Dust thou art, and unto dust shalt thou return.' All we go down to the dust; yet even at the grave we make our song: Alleluia, alleluia, alleluia.

> "Into thy hands, O merciful Savior, we commend thy servant George Henry Thomas. Acknowledge, we humbly beseech thee, a sheep of thine own fold, a lamb of thine own flock, a sinner of thine own redeeming. Receive him into the arms of thy mercy, into blessed rest of everlasting peace, and into the glorious company of the saints in light.

The pallbearers come forth from under the oak tree that arched over the Kellogg plot, raised the coffin on their shoulders, and slowly walked it into the open vault, as the reverend intoned,

In the midst of life we are in death;
of whom may we seek for succor,
but of thee, O Lord,
who for our sins art justly displeased?

Yet, O Lord God most holy, O Lord most mighty,
O holy and most merciful Savior,
deliver us not into the bitter pains of eternal death.

Thou knowest, Lord, the secrets of our hearts;
shut not thy merciful ears to our prayer;
but spare us, Lord most holy, O God most mighty,
O holy and merciful Savior,
thou most worthy Judge eternal.
Suffer us not, at our last hour,
through any pains of death, to fall from thee.

Colonel Willard and two members of Frances Kellogg's family stepped into the vault and said their goodbyes to the general, then returned, deliberately, to their places. The minister solemnly concluded:

In sure and certain hope of the resurrection to eternal life through our Lord Jesus Christ, we commend to Almighty God our brother George; and we commit his body to the ground; earth to earth, ashes to ashes, dust to dust. The Lord bless him and keep him, the Lord make his face to shine upon him and be gracious unto him, the Lord lift up his countenance upon him and give him peace. Amen

Suddenly, the former Army of the Cumberland color guard that had carried in the Stars and Stripes, and was still standing on a rise behind us, began firing together another fifty-three gun salute to their departed commander. Troy echoed San Francisco. One end of the country to the other.

The Funeral of General Thomas

When the last round echoed away, each regiment, in order, swung away from the gravesite and marched down one path or another to the entrances to Oakwood Cemetery. The President and his Cabinet members paused for a moment, and then walked deliberately back toward the crest of the hill they had ascended two hours before. The Kellogg family followed at a distance behind; they were not impressed by the President's attendance, adhering no doubt to Frances' wishes for men who had been disdainful or patronizing to her husband.

A band was playing military refrains in the distance. The crowds on the knolls were thinning. We left under overcast skies, left that beautiful cemetery and left General Thomas for the ages.

Time reveals all truths, and his memory, now being forgotten, will be restored.

The importance of all life lies not in our perfection but in our humanity, and it requires of those around us only what is each person's best, whatever that may be.

General Thomas stood for America: he let nothing stand in the way of his determination to bring all Americans together again.

May we do it as well as he.

May he rest in peace.

Epilogue

In 1879, a statue of General Thomas and his horse Ashes was erected in Washington, DC, a few blocks from the White House. It faces Virginia and Arlington Cemetery. Its dedication was the largest celebration in the history of the country's capitol; for half a day hundreds of regiments passed by.

Frances Thomas survived her husband by nineteen years, settling first in Troy and finally, after the dedication, in the house she built in Washington, DC whose east windows allowed an excellent view of her husband's statue.

She never again attended a military event.

www.ingramcontent.com/pod-product-compliance
Lightning Source LLC
Chambersburg PA
CBHW010253030726
47497CB00010BA/3196